WARRIOR'S VOW

"I am going to kill Wolf Who Hunts Smiling."

Touch the Sky's announcement struck everyone dumb, including Wolf Who Hunts Smiling and the Bull Whips. Little Horse gaped; even Arrow Keeper looked dumbfounded.

"You heard me straight," he went on. "His scaffold is as good as built. I will kill this murderer of Cheyenne, this traitor to his own tribe."

"What proof do you have?" Chief Gray Thunder demanded.

Touch the Sky shook his head. "Nothing I can place in your sash. But I swear by the four directions this one conspired with Big Tree. If he did not actually draw the blood of our dead companions, he at least allowed it to flow."

Gray Thunder met Touch the Sky's eyes. "I will brook no more talk of traitors and killing our own. Is this thing clear?"

Touch the Sky nodded once. "As you say, Gray Thunder," he finally replied. "No more talking."

11 CHEYENNE

SPIRIT PATH
JUDD COLE

LEISURE BOOKS   NEW YORK CITY

A LEISURE BOOK®

September 1994

Published by

Dorchester Publishing Co., Inc.
276 Fifth Avenue
New York, NY 10001

Printed in the United States of America.

Prologue

In the year the white man's winter-count called 1840, a band of Northern Cheyennes led by Chief Running Antelope was ambushed by blue-bloused soldiers near the North Platte.

When the last cavalry carbines finally fell silent, every Cheyenne lay dead or dying except Running Antelope's infant son, still clutched in the fallen chief's arms. Pawnee scouts were about to brain the child against a cottonwood when the lieutenant in charge interfered. He had the infant brought back to the Wyoming river-bend settlement of Bighorn Falls, near Fort Bates.

The child was adopted by John Hanchon and his barren wife Sarah, owners of the town's thriving mercantile store, which did a brisk business with nearby Fort Bates. The Hanchons named him Matthew and loved him as their own son. From the time he was old enough to be useful, he worked for his parents, stocking shelves and delivering orders to the fort and surrounding settlers.

Occasionally the young Cheyenne encountered hostile stares and remarks, especially from frontier hard cases passing through with Indian scalps dangling from their sashes. But his parents were well respected, and their love was strong enough to smooth the occasional rough places; aware that he was different from other settlers, the boy nonetheless grew up feeling accepted in his limited world.

Then came Matthew's sixteenth year and a tragic love that left him an outcast, welcome neither in the red man's world nor the white's.

Kristen was the daughter of the wealthy mustang rancher Hiram Steele. Surprising the young lovers in their secret meeting place, Steele ordered one of his wranglers to savagely beat the youth. Kristen's implacable father swore he'd kill Matthew if he caught them together again. Fearing for Matthew's life, Kristen lied and told the youth she never wanted to see him again.

To this new grief was soon added a serious threat to his parents. Seth Carlson, a young lieutenant from Fort Bates who had staked a claim to Kristen, delivered an ultimatum to the beleaguered youth: Either he left Bighorn Falls for good, or his adopted parents would lose their lucrative contract with Fort Bates—the lifeblood of their business.

Spirit Path

Saddened but determined, Matthew hardened his heart for whatever lay ahead. Then he pointed his bridle north toward the Powder River and Cheyenne country.

Captured by braves from Chief Yellow Bear's band, his hair-face clothing, language, and customs marked him as a traitor. He was sentenced to torture and death.

Lashed to a wagon wheel, he was mercilessly burned over glowing coals. Then, as a young buck named Wolf Who Hunts Smiling was about to kill him, old Arrow Keeper intervened. The tribal shaman, Arrow Keeper had recently experienced an important medicine dream. This vision foretold that an unknown Cheyenne youth, one who carried the mark of the warrior, would soon arrive at Yellow Bear's camp. The long-lost son of a great Cheyenne chief, this youth would eventually lead the entire *Shaiyena* nation in their last great victory against their enemies. Arrow Keeper spotted the mark—a mulberry-colored birthmark in the perfect shape of an arrowhead—buried past the unconscious youth's hairline.

At Arrow Keeper's insistence, the suspicious stranger's life was spared. But many in the tribe were infuriated when Arrow Keeper also insisted the youth must live with them—and even train as a warrior!

Arrow Keeper buried the hair-face name Matthew Hanchon in a hole and renamed the tall youth Touch the Sky. But the wily Wolf Who Hunts Smiling branded him a spy and a white man's dog. By deliberately stepping between Touch the Sky and the campfire, he announced his intention to someday kill his new enemy.

Touch the Sky earned a second formidable enemy in the older cousin of Wolf Who Hunts Smiling, Black Elk. The tribe's war leader, Black Elk saw the long, lingering glances Touch the Sky exchanged with Chief Yellow Bear's daughter Honey Eater. Black Elk planned to send the maiden the gift of marriage horses, and his hatred toward any rivals was great.

At first, up against two enemies covered with such hard bark, Touch the Sky seemed doomed. Only Arrow Keeper and Honey Eater were sympathetic. But neither dared to take his side openly for fear of making his miserable lot even worse. Black Elk led the warrior training, and the youth could not ride a pony, throw an ax, or even sharpen a knife correctly.

Taunted and brutalized by the other braves, he was eventually befriended by a sturdy youth named Little Horse. Through sheer determination to prove himself and finally belong somewhere, Touch the Sky eventually became one of the most able warriors in Yellow Bear's tribe.

But his enemies were clever and constantly turned appearances against him. Acceptance remained elusive, his enemies implacable. Forced by tribal pressures to accept Black Elk's gift of horses, Honey Eater married the war chief. But in her heart she could love only Touch the Sky.

Black Elk's cousin Wolf Who Hunts Smiling has long burned with ambition. He intends no less than a takeover of the tribe and the entire red nation, leading them in a war of extermination against the white invaders and their Indian spies.

Like Arrow Keeper, Touch the Sky has experienced the vision of his great destiny. Now Arrow Keeper has selected him for the long and difficult training as a shaman. For the old warrior knows that victory on the warpath alone will not be enough to save this young warrior from a hard and tragic fate.

Chapter One

"Place these words in your sashes, brothers," Tangle Hair said. "The music you are hearing right now comes from the hollowed-out leg bone of a dead Pawnee. And it is intended to taunt the ears of Touch the Sky and any who would raise their lances beside his."

The Bow String trooper fell silent, and the other braves seated around the fire nodded agreement. The flames sawed sharply in a sudden breeze, tracing the features of Tangle Hair, Touch the Sky, Little Horse, and the youngest among them, Two Twists.

Earlier, distant thunderheads had boiled over the Bighorn Mountains, and reefs of dark clouds had blown in from the north. Now, above the occasional muttering of distant thunder, they could hear the strange music

Tangle Hair spoke of: dull, atonal notes played with a slow precision that never varied. They emanated from the direction of the meat racks behind Black Elk's tipi—a favorite meeting place for the Cheyenne soldier society known as the Bull Whip Troop. Especially when the Whips were planning to do the hurt dance on an enemy.

And everyone in Gray Thunder's tribe knew who their main enemy within the tribe was: the tall Cheyenne who had arrived among them wearing the white man's shoes and the white man's stink. His shoes were long gone. But many still claimed the stink would never wash from him.

"He is playing the tune yet again," Little Horse said. The sturdy little warrior sat crushing coffee beans between two rocks. "It unstrings the horse's nerves and makes the infants cry. I had hoped the headmen would put a stop to it by now."

"They are afraid to," Touch the Sky said. "Many in the tribe are convinced by now that Medicine Flute has strong medicine. This tune, this lifeless thing which sounds like the wind rushing out of the neck when a pony is throat slashed. Wolf Who Hunts Smiling and others claim it can send an enemy running in fear."

Little Horse stopped his labors and glanced at his friend in the flickering firelight. Even seated cross-legged, Touch the Sky was clearly taller than the others. Choosing not to braid his hair, he wore it in long, loose black locks except over his eyes. There it was cut short to

11

free his vision. The warm moons were upon them, and like the other bucks, he wore only a clout and elkskin moccasins when in camp.

"Brother," Little Horse said, "I have seen the medicine you and Arrow Keeper can make. It is strong medicine, true medicine. This Medicine Flute, the warriors of his Spotted Ponies Clan are stout enough. Often one of them has worn the buffalo hat into battle. But tell me a thing. Do you believe Medicine Flute is marked out by the High Holy Ones for a shaman, as Wolf Who Hunts Smiling has begun to insist?"

Touch the Sky remained silent a long time, watching sparks fly up from the driftwood fire. Throughout Gray Thunder's summer camp, located at the fork of the Powder and Little Powder rivers, other clan fires glowed like bright eyes. Indian camps stayed active and noisy far into the night, there being no official bedtime. In the main clearing, young braves placed wagers on pony races, foot races, and wrestling contests. Children with miniature bows and willow-branch shields played at counting coups and taking prisoners. Old men stood in the doorways of the clan lodges, smoking fragrant red-willow bark and making brags about times they had raised the hatchet against Pawnees or Utes or the hair-faced blue soldiers.

"Arrow Keeper tells me that those truly marked for the gift of visions are rare," Touch the Sky finally replied. "Yet, I would be willing to believe that Medicine Flute has magic if Wolf Who Hunts Smiling were not behind the claim."

Little Horse immediately nodded, as did the others. "Count upon it, brother. Anything he touches has a bad smell to it. Long ago, before you even knew how to make a war whoop, he vowed to kill you. So did his lackey Swift Canoe when he blamed you for the death of his twin brother. And now Black Elk openly accuses you of wanting to put on the old moccasin with Honey Eater. All three are behind Black Elk's tipi right now. I fear whatever monster is born of this parley."

"Putting on the old moccasin" was a Cheyenne reference to an unmarried buck who desired a married woman. Everyone in the tribe knew how it was: Honey Eater, left alone when her father Chief Yellow Bear died, had been forced by the Cheyenne laws to marry.

But Touch the Sky, the one she loved, had been absent then; he had gone south to fight a battle for his white parents. Believing in her heart that Touch the Sky had deserted the tribe forever, she had reluctantly accepted Black Elk's gift of horses. Still today, Touch the Sky felt a sharp pang in his heart when he recalled riding back to camp to discover Honey Eater living in Black Elk's tipi and wearing the newlywed's bride shawl.

"Little Horse speaks straight arrow," Tangle Hair said. "Soon, I fear, Touch the Sky will once again have trouble firmly by the tail. But though his enemies are many, he no longer stands alone as he once did. I was there when he counted first coup at the Tongue River Battle. And I saw him stand shoulder to shoulder with you, Little Horse, when the white buffalo hiders attacked. They swarmed down on you like angry bees, but I swear by the four directions you two bucks fought like ten men!"

"And the elders," said the youth called Two Twists, who was named for his habit of wearing two braids. "Many of them would die for Touch the Sky. Like my old mother and grandmother, they were present at the hunt camp when Touch the Sky stood alone before an entire charge of Comanche and Kiowa raiders. They saw him make a deliberate target of himself to divert the attack."

All this praise embarrassed Touch the Sky, though it was true. But he held his face expressionless in the Indian way as he said, "It is good if I have these friends. For I have seen the determined glint in the eyes of Wolf Who Hunts Smiling and his cousin Black Elk. Neither buck is a warrior to trifle with.

"Black Elk, a simpler creature than his younger cousin, only wishes to kill me. He is hardened by jealousy, but he will not be treacherous toward his tribe. However, Wolf Who Hunts Smiling has the gleam of a terrible ambition sunk deep into his eyes. He knows that the old grandmothers now often sing the cure songs over Arrow Keeper; he knows our old shaman must soon cross over. He sees the clear division in our tribe between those who follow Arrow Keeper and the hotheaded younger bucks who think like the wild Dog Soldiers of our kin to the south. And in some way, this Medicine Flute will be part of this treachery."

Spirit Path

* * *

Far across the busy clearing, in the shifting shadows behind Black Elk's tipi, an impromptu council was being held.

The councilors included Black Elk, his younger cousin Wolf Who Hunts Smiling, and the latter's favorite lackey, Swift Canoe. Also present were Lone Bear, troop leader of the Bull Whip Soldier Society, and two highly feared Whips named Big Fist and Snake Eater.

Saying little, but the center of much of the attention, was a slender young buck named Medicine Flute, who had about 22 winters behind him. While the others took turns speaking, he continued to sound the flat, eerie notes of his Pawnee-bone flute.

"You are sure of this thing?" Wolf Who Hunts Smiling demanded.

The Bull Whip named Snake Eater nodded emphatically. "What? Am I suddenly a soft brain in his frosted years? Of course I am sure of this thing."

Wolf Who Hunts Smiling was too preoccupied to take offense at Snake Eater's arrogant tone. A bold scheme was hatching deep in the dark recesses of the young Cheyenne's mind—a scheme that was highly risky, yet potentially devastating to his enemies.

Wolf Who Hunts Smiling leaned closer to the fire, as if seeking clues in its roaring flames. He had an intelligent, wily face that befitted his name, with swift-as-minnow eyes constantly in motion—always on guard, Little Horse once said, for the ever expected attack.

Snake Eater had recently returned from a long visit to his brother, who had married a girl from the Southern Cheyenne living below the Platte. Living among those kinsmen was an Arapaho named Looks Beyond. In his youth he had gone to the white man's school in Denver. He had learned, like the Pawnee, to read the heavens and navigate by star charts.

"Tell us this thing again," Wolf Who Hunts Smiling said. "This thing with the fire-tailed star."

A calumet lay on the ground between Snake Eater and Big Fist. Snake Eater, swollen with the sense of his own importance, picked up the long-stemmed pipe and stoked it to life with a piece of glowing punk. Only after he had smoked and set the pipe back down did he deign to speak.

"This Looks Beyond, he can predict events that will occur in the heavens. He knows that soon, when the dog constellation lines up with the dawn star in the east, a huge, bright star with a flaming tale will shoot across the western heavens. The palefaces call it a comet."

Black Elk scowled impatiently. He was irritated equally by such pointless talk and Medicine Pipe's monotonous music. He looked particularly fierce in the stark firelight. One of his ears was a dead, leathery flap hanging from his head by buckskin thread. It had been severed in battle by a bluecoat saber. Black Elk had sewn it back on himself.

"Only women and old men talk like this merely to hear themselves speak! Of what importance can it be that this Arapaho predicts events in the heavens?"

"Be patient, cousin," Wolf Who Hunts Smiling said. "I will soon crack the shell and dig down to the meat."

Wolf Who Hunts Smiling glanced over at Medicine Flute. The young buck kept his heavy-lidded gaze focused into the flames while he played his eerie music.

"How soon," Wolf Who Hunts Smiling asked Snake Eater, "will this fiery star blaze across the heavens?"

"Within the next few sleeps."

"Good."

Now Wolf Who Hunts Smiling again looked at Medicine Flute. "Brother," he said, "do you believe that White Man Runs Him possesses strong medicine?"

Wolf Who Hunts Smiling had used his favorite name for Touch the Sky. He also occasionally called him Woman Face—after his former white man's habit of letting his feelings show in his face, a trait despised by Indians.

Now Medicine Flute finally lowered his grisly instrument. Still gazing into the fire with his unvarying stare, he suddenly laughed.

"Medicine? Add all his medicine to an arrow, and you will have an arrow. Any fool can put the trance glaze over his eyes, quicken his breathing, and speak in mystic phrases of visions. There are always enough fools to believe."

"You seem to know deception well. Is this what you do?"

17

Medicine Flute smiled, but wisely said nothing except to repeat, "There are always fools enough."

"Good. Good. For very soon you are going to make an announcement. A prediction about this comet."

"For what purpose?" Black Elk demanded.

"For the purpose of winning the people away from Arrow Keeper and his assistant, White Man Runs Him. Cousin, you have eyes to see. Surely you understand that he who controls a tribe's medicine also controls the tribe?"

Black Elk's scowl softened somewhat as he began to catch the drift of his cousin's thinking. He had failed to understand his cousin's reference to controlling the tribe. All he cared about was the part about winning the people away from Touch the Sky. How many times had he caught Honey Eater crying for the tall buck? How many lingering glances had they traded? Touch the Sky's growing reputation as a shaman made it increasingly difficult to persecute him. If this bold plan worked, the intruder might once again be reduced to the status of a white man's dog.

As for Medicine Flute, this was all much to his liking. He had sniffed opportunity from the very moment that Wolf Who Hunts Smiling had first befriended him. The clever youth was lazy, and though he was a trained warrior, fighting and the hard life of the warpath held no appeal for him. Everyone knew that the life of a respected medicine man, in contrast, could be very pleasant indeed. Never did a powerful shaman lack for meat in his racks or fine buffalo robes.

"Cousin," Black Elk finally said, "I have ears for these words. Speak more of them."

Less than a stone's throw away, at the rear of Black Elk's darkened tipi, the hide cover had been lifted away from the pole. Crouched nervously in the dark, her frightened heart pounding in her throat, Honey Eater took in every treacherous word.

Besides her anger at this latest plot to destroy Touch the Sky, she felt an even stronger emotion gnawing at her: fear. Black Elk and his spies had made it virtually impossible for her to even look at Touch the Sky, much less communicate with him.

But communicate she must. They had sworn their love for each other, and more than once he had shed blood protecting her. His enemies were her enemies—even if one of the enemies was her own husband.

Crouched there in the darkness, trembling at her fear of Black Elk's monstrous rage, she nonetheless resolved to somehow warn Touch the Sky.

Just south of runoff-swollen Bear Creek, about one-half sleep's ride from Gray Thunder's camp, the Quohada Comanche battle leader named Big Tree and a score of his followers had established a cold camp. Not long before they had left behind the pumice plains, flowering yuccas, and low-hanging pods of mesquite that surrounded their permanent camp in New Mexico's Blanco Canyon.

19

Their magnificent horses were descended from stock introduced further south by the Spanish. Normally, when on the warpath like this, their mounts were kept hobbled foreleg to rear to keep them close. But now they had been turned loose to graze the lush grass bordering Bear Creek.

Big Tree planned to ride out soon for a lone night scout of the area. He caught up his mount, a stocking-footed chestnut, and cinched tight his stolen Texas stock saddle with its bare tree. A roadrunner skin dangled from his horse's tail. It was the good-luck charm of the Comanche tribe.

Big Tree was large for a Comanche, though he was bandy-legged and clumsy on foot like most men of his tribe. Once mounted, however, Comanche warriors could quickly demonstrate why they were called the natural jockeys of the plains—especially Big Tree's Quohada, or Antelope-eater, Band, the famous Red Raiders of the barren Staked Plain.

Several of the packhorses were reserved for hauling huge animal skins filled with pulque, the bitter cactus liquor brewed by the Comanches. One had been untied and liquor-filled gourds were making the rounds.

Big Tree moved easily among his men, accepting a sip here, exchanging a friendly insult there. Because Comanche men admired skill in battle above all else, Big Tree was a respected leader. He alone in the entire Comanche nation could ride 300 yards—and launch 20 arrows—in the time it took a bluecoat soldier to load and fire his carbine. Once, while dead drunk, Big Tree had astounded his fellow braves by launching the last of ten arrows before the first had reached its target.

"Cheyenne guts will string our next bows!" someone shouted, and a cheer rose above the snuffling of the horses.

"*Matanlos!*" came the cry in Spanish. "Kill them!"

"Remember those who can never be mentioned again!" someone else shouted. This was a reference to the braves killed when the tall Cheyenne's band had defeated them and regained their kidnapped women and children—including the slender young beauty Big Tree had been dreaming of bulling. That skirmish had killed the slave trader Juan Aragon and his comancheros. It had also sent many good Comanches and Kiowa allies under. In the survivors' rush to escape, their bodies had been left behind. And by strict custom, any Comanche whose body had not been recovered could never be mentioned by name again.

"Do we attack tonight, Quohada?" the warrior named Rain in His Face demanded.

Big Tree shook his head. No fires were permitted, but a full moon had emerged from the clouds. It limned his features in a stark, silver-white glow like fox fire. He wore a tall shako hat with silver conchos captured from a Mexican officer. Around his neck hung a necklace of dried and blackened human ears. Moonlight reflected from the bits of broken mirror glass embedded in his shield to blind his enemies in the sun.

"Attack, no. Not yet, not now. They are too strong in their main camp, and these Cheyennes, they keep too many dogs trained to bark at an enemy's smell. We cannot hope to surprise them. But I will ride out tonight to study the lay of their camp and the outlying herds. We did not ride this far to die foolishly, but to profit by our enemy's loss. And truly, they are rich in fine ponies."

Big Tree jabbed a stick into the ground and bent it forward. "When the angle of the Dipper matches this stick, I ride. Be patient, stout bucks! Let these scalp-taking fools die for the sheer glory of death. We will not only exact our revenge, but live to enjoy it.

"The superstitious Pawnees claim this tall Cheyenne is a shaman. They say he can summon the grizzly and conjure up insane white men. I say his brain will roast like any other. And I swear by the earth I live on, each of us will taste a piece of it!"

Chapter Two

One sleep after the Cheyenne Bull Whips had met to plan Touch the Sky's downfall, the Renewal of the Sacred Medicine Arrows was held in the central camp clearing.

Arrow Keeper and Touch the Sky presided. Both wore their finest warbonnets, elaborately quilled moccasins, beadwork leggings, and leather shirts. This annual ceremony, involving the entire tribe, was conducted to remind the people of the thought of the Arrows.

The four sacred Medicine Arrows, protected by Arrow Keeper with his very life, symbolized the fate of the *Shaiyena* nation. Whatever fate befell the Arrows would also befall the tribe. One Cheyenne spilling the blood of another, or otherwise violating the Cheyenne laws, stained the Arrows and thus the entire tribe. The High

23

Holy Ones required that these four blue-and-yellow ceremonial arrows be kept forever sweet and clean, forever protected from enemy hands. And when Arrow Keeper crossed over to the Land of Ghosts, Touch the Sky would become the new Keeper.

The Renewal, also held before battle, cleansed the Arrows of any stains accumulated during the previous moons. Each adult with 12 or more winters lined up to make an offering to the Arrows.

Taking turns, Arrow Keeper and Touch the Sky chanted the long Renewal Prayer while the gifts were piled up around the stump that held the Arrows. Arrow Keeper's failing health required Touch the Sky to lead most of the ceremony. Several times, Honey Eater's eyes met his. She hoped to send him a signal about the plan against him. But each time, before she could attempt to convey a warning, he glanced hastily away. Touch the Sky had learned well the danger to Honey Eater if Black Elk caught them looking at each other.

The last clan had filed by, and Arrow Keeper had wrapped the Medicine Arrows in their coyote-fur pouch. The closing prayer was chanted to the rhythmic backdrop of snake teeth rattling in dried gourds. Arrow Keeper was about to dismiss the tribe, clearing the central square, when a voice rang out.

"Fathers and brothers! Have ears for my words!"

Touch the Sky felt a sharp point of apprehension when he recognized the voice of Wolf

24

Who Hunts Smiling. Everyone stopped, turned, and stared at the speaker. Huge driftwood fires made the clearing as bright as day.

None could help noticing that Wolf Who Hunts Smiling wore no coup feathers in his bonnet. Though by right of combat he had earned many, the Council of Forty had stripped him of his right to wear them. This happened after Wolf Who Hunts Smiling bribed an old grandmother; he convinced her to claim she'd had a vision requiring Touch the Sky to "set up a pole," to drive sharp hooks through his breast and hang suspended from them all day. Arrow Keeper finally exposed the plot, but only after Touch the Sky had suffered for hours.

"True it is," Wolf Who Hunts Smiling said, "I wear no coup feathers. But I have scalped Pawnees, Crows, Comanches, and Kiowas. I was the first to shed enemy blood at the Tongue River Battle. I have slain hair-faced sellers of strong water and paleface militiamen who would take our land. Never has Wolf Who Hunts Smiling cowered in his tipi when his brothers were on the warpath! So hear me now!"

Touch the Sky and Arrow Keeper exchanged troubled glances. Their faces were painted for the ceremony. Bright claybank reds and yellows and blacks made them look fierce and eerie in the flickering flames.

"I have long been expecting this moment," Arrow Keeper said in a voice meant for Touch the Sky alone. "Now will the ambitious young buck challenge the lead bulls!"

"Fathers and brothers!" Wolf Who Hunts Smiling continued. "I will not mince words like a timid girl, but state the case boldly. Our tribe needs new and more powerful medicine! How many babes died of the red-speckled cough during these last cold moons? And what of these white buffalo hiders arriving almost daily to destroy our herds or these blue-bloused pony soldiers building their towns in the midst of our best hunting grounds?

"Is it not as clear as a blood trail in new snow? Our medicine is weak. A tribe with weak medicine is a dead tribe!"

There were certainly some grains of truth mixed up in the chaff of these complaints. All listened. It was Little Horse who first answered.

"Wolf Who Hunts Smiling's sudden interest in strong medicine should be scanned. This from him who bribes addled old grandmothers into making a mockery of true visions and the straight word!"

"I have ears for this," Tangle Hair agreed, and several of his Bow String troop brothers chorused assent. "No one here questions the fighting skill or courage of Wolf Who Hunts Smiling. He is a stranger to fear. But sadly, he is also a stranger to truth."

"A stranger to truth?" Black Elk said. "Do you deny that we have lost many infants to sickness? That the paleface hiders are destroying our buffalo herds? Do Little Horse and Tangle Hair claim the forts cropping up like mushrooms all around us are merely *odjib*, things of smoke? Bad medicine is at work against us!"

Spirit Path

Now there was a shout of support from the Bull Whips. Their reaction emboldened Wolf Who Hunts Smiling, whose power as a speaker was greatly admired. Even as the young Cheyenne swelled up to speak, Arrow Keeper leaned close and whispered to Touch the Sky.

"Now you will hear me lavishly praised before he sticks his blade deep and gives it a twist."

"Fathers and brothers!" Wolf Who Hunts Smiling said. "I speak only words that you may pick up and place in your sashes. Old Arrow Keeper here is a truly great Cheyenne! He has strewn his enemy's bones throughout the land of the Bighorn Sheep. Count his coup feathers! Once his medicine—like his wisdom—was as vast as the plains, as strong as a winter-rested bear.

"But time is a bird, and that bird has long been on the wing. How many snows has Arrow Keeper seen? How many spring melts, how many greenings of the new grass? He has served his tribe well. But even the mightiest trees eventually lose their sap."

Again many nodded inwardly, if not openly, at the truth of these words. Now Wolf Who Hunts Smiling trained his gleaming black-agate eyes on Touch the Sky.

"The best proof of Arrow Keeper's tangled brain is his selection of our next tribal shaman and Keeper of the Arrows. Clearly this one here is useless. Yes, he knows the words of the ceremonies. But how can a Cheyenne shaman be raised by white men? Would badgers follow a cow or geese fly with the buzzard?"

Arrow Keeper had deliberately held his silence. But Touch the Sky had supped full of this two-faced talk.

"Listen to this Wolf Who Hunts Smiling! How many times has he shed the blood of his own, sullying the Arrows? How many times has he shown open disrespect to our laws and to Arrow Keeper, a shaman whose medicine is feared and respected from where I stand now to the sun's resting place? How many times has this wily Wolf Who Hunts Smiling placed his own narrow ambitions over the good of his tribe?

"And now, listen to this jay's deceptive chatter! Little Horse spoke straight arrow just now. This sudden interest in strong medicine has the putrid smell of a foul plot to it."

"You speak of plots!" Black Elk fumed. "You who plot to steal the women of your betters!"

Everyone present knew he meant Honey Eater, and many present stared at her. Refusing to be shamed by their stares, she boldly held her head high and met all comers fully in the eye—just as she had done when Black Elk once cut off her beautiful braid as a public mark of shame.

"It remains to be seen," Touch the Sky said calmly, leveling an unblinking stare at Black Elk and his cousin, "just who my betters are. On that score, deeds will soon enough speak for words. As for stealing women, they are not blankets or trade knives. Our women have hearts of their own, nor can a man steal that which is his by right."

Spirit Path

At these last words the fury in Black Elk's eyes was frightening to behold. But before he could retort, Spotted Tail of the Bow Strings shouted out, "Wolf Who Hunts Smiling! With one brief speech you have denied the medicine of both Arrow Keeper and Touch the Sky. So then, having stripped your tribe of medicine men, who would you propose for our shaman? Perhaps your loyal shadow, the holy man Swift Canoe?"

His words brought a hearty ripple of laughter. Swift Canoe was a capable enough warrior, given clear orders. But it was common knowledge that his brain was far slower than his name.

His sneer never wavering, Wolf Who Hunts Smiling waited for the laughter to abate. Then he said, "Enjoy your little jokes! Your jests, Spotted Tail, are as faint as your manhood. I, my cousin Black Elk, and the rest of the Bull Whips mark well the faces turned toward me now in mockery! The worm turns slowly, people, but it does indeed turn.

"Now I present the one Cheyenne among us who is truly possessed of strong and true medicine. Medicine Flute! Come forward and tell the people what you have told me."

All heads craned to watch as the slim young buck with the mysterious, heavy-lidded gaze came forward. He glided out from the shadows at the edge of the clearing like a wraith. As always, he carried his odd leg-bone flute.

The tribe fell so silent that nothing could be heard but the wind blowing through the

29

trees, the fires crackling. Medicine Flute already enjoyed a certain status among his clan as a visionary. His odd appearance and manner marked him as different and exotic. And when he spoke, the hollow ghost tone of his voice, combined with his fixed, unvarying stare, commanded the attention of all.

"There is music in the spheres, destiny in a handful of sand. Those who claim to see visions are many, but few ever tread the upward path of the Spirit Way. Fewer still produce true acts of strong medicine. Any fool can clap his hands at the moment a tree begins to fall down and then say he clapped that tree down. But who among you will promise well ahead of the event to set the largest star in the heavens on fire and then trail it, burning, across the sky?"

This claim to such power was so preposterous that many openly gaped or laughed.

"Laugh loud so we can remember the skeptics! You who scoff live in the life of the little day. Within the next few sleeps," Medicine Flute said, "I will do this thing."

"And I," Tangle Hair said, "will make the Powder run backward!"

"I will run atop the wind!" Spotted Tail threw in, and many laughed.

But Touch the Sky and Arrow Keeper did not share in the general mirth. Despite this impossible claim, they knew Wolf Who Hunts Smiling far too well. Serious trouble was afoot.

"How will you do this thing?" someone demanded.

Spirit Path

But Medicine Flute was done speaking. Now, he calmly lifted his flute to his lips. A moment later the dull notes of his eerie music drifted out over the people, hushing them.

Only once, as he played, did his eyes move from their ever fixed point somewhere on the horizon. For a few heartbeats they fixed instead on Touch the Sky; a slow, mocking smile divided Medicine Flute's face.

On the morning following Medicine Flute's bold prediction, Wolf Who Hunts Smiling rode into incredible good luck.

He had ridden out alone well to the south, training a new pony he had acquired in a trade with a brave of the Broken Lance Clan. He was practicing turns and reverse charges in a grassy draw north of Bear Creek. Abruptly, two Cheyenne riders appeared, racing toward him from the south with their braids flying out behind them. The red and black streamers tied to their ponies' tails told him they were Bull Whips. When they had come even closer, he recognized Big Fist and Snake Eater. He remembered that both were on scouting duty.

"Brother!" Big Fist greeted him. "Now our warriors are in for some rough sport! Comanches are camped just across Bear Creek. And their faces are painted black!"

"They are led by the trick rider Big Tree," Snake Eater added.

Big Fist said, "Finally they have arrived to avenge our victory against them and Juan Aragon's comancheros."

"How many?"

"A sizable war party, though clearly not enough to attack our main camp."

Wolf Who Hunts Smiling only nodded, holding his own thoughts close. Long had the wily young Cheyenne waited for an opportunity to speak with Big Tree. After all, he had already made a private treaty with the fierce Blackfoot renegade named Sis-ki-dee to the north. Like Sis-ki-dee, Big Tree struck Wolf Who Hunts Smiling as a brave of reckless courage and ruthless ambitions—two traits the power-starved Cheyenne could greatly appreciate.

"We must hurry back to camp with this word," Big Fist said. Wolf Who Hunts Smiling nodded again, watching them resume their hard ride to the north.

But as soon as they were specks on the horizon, he pulled a piece of dirty white cloth from his parfleche and tied it to his lance. Lifting this makeshift truce flag high, he pointed bridle toward Bear Creek and urged his mount to a gallop.

"Look here, Big Tree," the Comanche named Rain in His Face said. "We have been discovered! And our enemy has sent a word-bringer to parley."

The two Quohadas had ridden forward from their trail camp near the creek, scouting for enemies. Sitting their ponies behind a rocky bluff, they watched the lone Cheyenne approach.

32

Big Tree squinted, more curious than worried. It was not the Cheyenne way to negotiate like this with a sworn enemy.

"It is common knowledge that your mother ruts with Comanches!" he called out in his own tongue when the stranger was close enough to hear. At the other man's blank face, he repeated the insult in Kiowa, Spanish, and finally English.

"Of course," the new arrival responded in the stiff but clear English he had learned while a prisoner of the bluecoats. He added a furtive, cynical smile. "Every brave in my tribe mounts her. Why not yours, too?"

These irreverent and unexpected words made Big Tree's jaw open. He stared at Rain in His Face. Both were surprised. Normally a Cheyenne—haughty and emotional, like their Sioux cousins—was quick to take insult.

A moment later, Big Tree sensed a kindred spirit and laughed with hearty appreciation.

"Load a pipe," he called over to Rain in His Face. "I would smoke with this wily Cheyenne!"

"You are Big Tree. Your skill with the bow is widely know. I am called Wolf Who Hunts Smiling," the Cheyenne said in English.

"A wolf who hunts smiling usually has his nose to a spoor. This is true?"

"Of course. So does a Comanche who rides this far north from his desert home. And perhaps we are both sniffing the same spoor— that of a tall young buck who calls himself a shaman?"

So far Big Tree liked the drift of the conversation. But he showed nothing in his face. The Cheyenne's words could all be a piece of clever deception. He slid a Colt revolving-cylinder pistol from his sash. Calmly, in a deliberate show of indifference, he charged the bore and seated a bullet, driving it home. When the chambers were all loaded, he capped them. Only when he was finished did he deign to speak again. He still held the weapon, though it wasn't aimed at the Cheyenne.

"Why should I trust you, scalp-taker? Our two tribes have raised the hatchet against each other since Wolf Creek. Why should I not simply flay your soles?"

This was a reference to a favorite Comanche cruelty: skinning the soles off an enemy's feet, then setting him loose in the wilderness to walk.

"Because you, too, hate this tall buck as much as I do. You must, after what he did to humiliate your warriors. Why deny it? Your braves are good fighters, but you are not enough to attack a strong Cheyenne camp. Together, however, we can defeat this shaman. Then we can form an empire. We can control the plains from the Land of the Grandmother in the north to the Rio Bravo in the south."

Still, Big Tree showed nothing in his face. But he liked the talk more and more.

"What is it you intend?" he said. "To kill him?"

"If possible. But that has proven as difficult as galloping in sand. Almost as good to expose

34

him as a make-believe shaman."

Briefly, Wolf Who Hunts Smiling explained his plan to discredit Touch the Sky's magic, with the cooperation of Medicine Flute and Big Tree.

The Comanche liked the plot even better than an outright kill. It appealed to his warped sense of irony. And it would shame and humiliate the tall young buck, who clearly suffered from an excess of pride.

Besides, no private treaty with a Cheyenne would be binding forever. If the plan failed, another might work.

"How can I measure the depth of your sincerity?" Big Tree finally asked.

"What is it you would have?"

Big Tree held the Cheyenne's eyes with his own. For a moment he recalled the young Cheyenne woman with skin like glistening copper. How cleverly she had pitted the Kiowa leader Hairy Wolf and the Comanche leader Iron Eyes against each other! How cleverly she had driven both men mad with lust and made each feel she secretly preferred him. That division had led to their deaths. And Big Tree also knew she was the woman of the tall shaman.

"What is it I would have? Nothing less than your pony herd."

This was steep. But Wolf Who Hunts Smiling never once flinched. "If I help you gain them, will you then help me?"

"Gladly. Tell me what I must do. But I say to you now, and you may pick these words up

35

and carry them with you, I am not content to merely give the lie to this buck's reputation as a shaman. I intend to roast his brain and eat it."

Chapter Three

"Brother," Little Horse said, "I swear by the four directions, if Medicine Flute plays his tune one more time I will go Wendigo!"

Three sleeps had passed since Medicine Flute made his arrogant prediction. Despite the general feeling that the young buck was merely boasting, each night had seen most of the clan circles gathered in the main clearing, with a close eye on the heavens.

True, the Bull Whip scouts had reported a Comanche war party at Bear Creek. But even blue soldiers with big-thundering wagon guns were afraid to attack Gray Thunder's summer camp. More people were more frightened about this bold prediction than by a few marauding Comanches.

With sister sun only a ruddy afterglow on the

western horizon, the people were gathering yet again. A few called out jokingly to friends and clan relatives, "Tonight will be the night! Eyes to the skies, Cheyenne!"

And during all of it, Medicine Flute sat unperturbed, playing his eerie, monotonous song. His parents were dead, and he had sent the gift of horses to no woman. His tipi stood with those of the rest of his Spotted Ponies Clan directly across the clearing from Touch the Sky's. Now and then, as he played, Medicine Flute lifted mocking eyes toward Touch the Sky.

Little Horse glanced around the camp. "Buck, have you seen Wolf Who Hunts Smiling?"

Touch the Sky shook his head. He knelt to touch spark to a small pile of punk and kindling, starting a tiny fire under the wood of the cooking tripod outside his tipi.

"No, I have not seen him. And do you not find it curious, brother, that he has ridden out so close to nightfall—especially with Comanches nearby? And why now, when he should be in camp to enjoy his moment of glory if Medicine Flute pulls a flaming star across the sky?"

Little Horse watched his friend closely. "Curious indeed, Cheyenne. Is something in the wind?"

For a moment Touch the Sky interrupted his labors to gaze out toward the hostile shadows lengthening beyond the camp. A light tickle, like an insect crawling, moved up his spine.

"Brother," he said, "tell me this. When is something not in the wind?"

He fell silent, and the flat notes of Medicine Flute's tune reached them once again.

Wolf Who Hunts Smiling had no idea when the white man's comet was due to pass. He knew only that Big Tree was growing impatient to strike. So they had settled on this night, when herd guard duty was the responsibility of Wolf Who Hunts Smiling's rivals, the Bow String troopers.

The main pony herd, nearly 200 head of excellent mustangs, had been captured during long and difficult spring hunts in the high rimland of the Little Bighorns. The horses had been broken in and marked by their various owners. He himself had three on his string besides the paint he rode. All would have to be lost or he risked exposing his treachery to his own tribe.

But ponies could be replaced. If the raid that night indeed won Big Tree over to his cause, three ponies would be a small price to pay for destroying Touch the Sky. His destruction was assured if Big Tree cooperated now and in the near future.

Wolf Who Hunts Smiling's plan for tonight, as always with him, was simple and bold. He had already described the location of the herd to Big Tree. They were grouped north of camp in a natural sink where forage was good and fresh water covered a rock bed. There was no corral, only four mounted guards—one riding each flank.

It was critical that no shots be fired during the raid, or the main camp would be alerted.

So Wolf Who Hunts Smiling had based his plan on simple treachery.

He approached the herd on the south flank. He was immediately challenged by the vigilant Bow String sentry, Born in Snow. Wolf Who Hunts Smiling identified himself.

"Why are you here?" Born in Snow asked suspiciously. There was no love lost between the Bow Strings and Wolf Who Hunts Smiling's Bull Whip troop. "Everyone in camp is watching the heavens to see your new shaman count coup on the stars."

"Mock all you wish. They will not be disappointed, buck. Nor will you. As for me, I am indifferent to shows of magic. I have come to cut out my new buckskin and ride him. The strong one with the yellow mane. Have you seen this one?"

Born in Snow frowned in the silver-white moonlight. His pony started and pricked her ears toward a line of nearby sandstone shoulders. Born in Snow glanced in that direction.

"When did you develop this love of night riding, Bull Whip? Do you have foolish plans to count first coup on the Comanches?"

Wolf Who Hunts Smiling scowled. "If you know my name, Bow String, then you also know I am not one to play the big Indian with. I asked if you have seen my pony, and I expect a civil answer."

Born in Snow scowled back. But despite his suspicions, he did not wish to force Wolf Who Hunts Smiling up onto his hind legs. He tugged on his pony's hackamore, turning it away from the sandstone shoulders. He pointed off toward the far side of the natural sink.

As Born in Snow started to speak, Wolf Who Hunts Smiling slid the Colt Model 1855 rifle from its scabbard. Gripping the muzzle, he swung the wooden stock hard into the side of the guard's head. Born in Snow grunted once, then slumped, sliding to the ground like a heavy bag of grain.

Wolf Who Hunts Smiling imitated the hoot of an owl. A few heartbeats later, several shadows slid forward from the deeper darkness behind the sandstone shoulders.

Big Tree and his warriors had smoked their ponies and their clothing in cedar-and-sage fires to cover their unfamiliar smell and avoid spooking the mustangs. While they slipped around the fortified Cheyenne camp, silence was also critical. So the Comanches had muffled their horse's heads with blankets. Now they removed them.

"Wait here," Wolf Who Hunts Smiling told the war leader. "I will send the others back one by one. If you value your scalp, do nothing to scatter the horses."

But Big Tree barely nodded. He was busy watching as Rain in His Face and another brave dismounted. To conserve ammunition and kill without noise, the stealthy Comanches wore deadly rawhide-wrapped rocks looped around their wrists with thongs. There was a fast, hollow thud, then another and another, as they beat the fallen Cheyenne's head to a bloody pulp. When they finished, Big Tree met the eyes of Wolf Who Hunts Smiling. The Comanche grinned wide.

"We are killing your own, Cheyenne. Will you beg us to stop?"

Wolf Who Hunts Smiling had indeed flinched at the first blows. But he hardened his heart until it was all stone with no soft place left in it. Loyalty to his tribe had finally given way completely to his ambition and his long-seething hatred for Touch the Sky. Truly, Touch the Sky was marked out as an obstacle to his destiny. The business tonight was not pleasant, but was necessary. A weak man, Wolf Who Hunts Smiling reminded himself, had no business trying to be a leader of men.

"The day I beg for anything," Wolf Who Hunts Smiling replied, "is the same day a grizzly will mate with a horse."

Wolf Who Hunts Smiling urged his paint toward the west flank. The guard there was Stands on His Sash.

"Brother, lower that rifle. I am no enemy!" Wolf Who Hunts Smiling greeted him. "We have trouble! I came to cut one of my ponies out of the herd, and I found Born in Snow lying hurt on the ground. Evidently his horse threw him and he struck his head. He is still breathing. You ride back to him while I bring help from camp."

Stands on His Sash nodded and chucked up his pony, racing for Born in Snow's position. Then, his heart hard as flint, Wolf Who Hunts Smiling proceeded to send the rest of the herd guards to a hard death among the waiting Comanches.

Night had descended over the Powder River Valley like a dark cape unfurling. Touch the Sky and Little Horse lingered over the last of juicy elk steaks dripping marrow fat. They spoke of inconsequential matters.

Suddenly a cry rose from the center of camp. "Look! Look to the sky! Maiyun protect us. Look!"

Touch the Sky did look. He craned his neck and stared up toward a star-spangled sky dotted with thousands of glittering pinpoints. A falling star, he told himself, nothing more. But at first, looking at the wrong quadrant of the heavens, he noticed absolutely nothing out of the ordinary, not even a falling star.

Then his eyes scanned in another direction, and suddenly his blood seemed to reverse its flow in his veins.

A huge, magnificent, bluish-green ball of fire trailing a long and brilliant tail arced through the heavens. It seemed so close that Touch the Sky almost believed he could reach up and pluck it from the dark dome of the sky.

"Look! Look!"

"Medicine Flute spoke straight arrow! Look, only look! He has moved the very heavens with his great medicine!"

"This time Wolf Who Hunts Smiling spoke from one side of his mouth. This is truly big medicine. Even old Arrow Keeper never set a star on fire!"

Comments such as these flew through the camp. Some of the more superstitious Cheyennes even became hysterical and fell upon the ground, stupefied. Children bawled in fright, dogs howled, and old grandmothers sang their ancient prayers.

"Brother," Little Horse's voice said beside him, amazement clear in his tone, "how can this thing be? How?"

Slowly, still watching the wondrous spectacle blaze across the sky, Touch the Sky shook his head.

"Buck, I know not. But count upon it, the Cheyenne winter-count will call this The Time When Medicine Flute Burned A Star."

Touch the Sky was referring to the pictographs that Indian elders made to record the major events of each year. A moment later, with shouts still ringing throughout camp, Arrow Keeper moved up next to the two youths.

"Father," Little Horse said, "how did Medicine Flute perform this amazing magic?"

Arrow Keeper, too, glanced overhead as the miraculous vision cleared the last part of the visible sky.

"What we are seeing is indeed amazing," Arrow Keeper said. "So, in its own way, is the weaving of a spider's web or the foaling of a mare. However, that it is also magic, I am not so sure."

"But, Father, you heard Medicine Flute predict this thing before it even happened."

"I did, little brother. I also heard the worst liar in our camp call him forward to announce it. When a Pawnee raises one hand in friend-ship, ignore it. Instead, watch the hand hidden behind his back."

"Speaking of liars and hands hidden behind the back," Touch the Sky said, glancing around, "where is Wolf Who Hunts Smiling? What could be so important that he would miss his new brother's great triumph?"

At that same moment, the sound of horses whinnying reached them from north of camp, where the herd was bunched. Perhaps, Touch the Sky told himself, it was only the horses reacting to the strange celestial phenomenon.

Then his eyes met Arrow Keeper's in the firelight. And when the old man nodded slightly, Touch the Sky realized that the senior shaman felt the same hunch his apprentice did.

Touch the Sky had not yet returned his best pony, a tough little bay with a white blaze on her forehead, to graze with the others in the herd. Instead, she was tethered behind his tipi, cropping the bunch grass.

"Brother," he said to Little Horse, "keep your eyes open for Wolf Who Hunts Smiling. I want to know when he returns and from what direc-tion."

"As good as done, buck. But where are you going?"

Again Touch the Sky glanced at Arrow Keep-er. "To check on the ponies."

Before he caught up his pony, he lifted the hide entrance flap and slipped inside his tipi. He stirred up the embers in the firepit. By their light he slid his Sharps percussion-action rifle from under the buffalo robe that protected it from dew at night. He made sure there was a bullet behind the loading gate and dry powder in the charger. He capped the piece and stepped outside.

The blazing wonder had finally cleared this section of the sky. But still the people stood in groups, clamoring at the amazing feat. As he grabbed his pony's mane and swung up onto her, Touch the Sky again saw Medicine Flute across the way, calmly playing his legbone flute.

Touch the Sky had just cleared the sandstone shoulders when he recognized the sound of pounding hooves. Ahead, in the ghostly moonlight, he saw the pony herd racing to the west in a tightly bunched group—Comanche warriors pointing them!

He had been riding with the butt plate of his Sharps resting on his thigh. Now he raised the piece and fired a warning shot to summon warriors from camp, then slid his rifle into the rawhide scabbard sewn to his rope rigging.

A moment later his pony nearly stumbled on a grisly sight: the four Cheyenne herd guards heaped together on the south flank of the natural corral. They had been savagely brained, their heads cruelly battered so hard they looked like squashed melons. Nor had the Comanches, who scorned scalp-taking, neglected their penchant for horrible mutilations. Each brave wore his genitals crammed into his mouth, and the coiled white ropes of their intestines had been pulled through slits in their bellies.

Spirit Path

Hearing the thud of a hoof, Touch the Sky looked up even as he slid an arrow from his fox-skin quiver and notched it in his bow.

Wolf Who Hunts Smiling sat his pony only an arm's length away. He held his Colt rifle aimed at Touch the Sky, who in turn aimed his arrow at the other brave's chest.

"You! Why are you riding this way, braggart warrior?" Touch the Sky demanded. "You and your cousin Black Elk tire me with your endless boasting about how you will grease your enemy's bones with war paint. And now, under your nose, Comanches escape in the opposite direction with our ponies!"

But Wolf Who Hunts Smiling had seen the comet pass. And now he knew that Touch the Sky's glory—as well as that of the old soft brain, Arrow Keeper—would soon be as dead as those Bow String troopers. In fact, he thought, a little more pressure on his trigger right now, and—

"If you do it," the young shaman said, easily reading his enemy's face, "my dead fingers will let fly this arrow. Look at it! I hardened it twice in fire and filed those points on pumice. This arrow would drop a black bear."

Wolf Who Hunts Smiling loosed a long, harsh laugh. He slid his finger outside the trigger guard.

"As you say, shaman. Why should I waste a good bullet? Soon the people will worship Medicine Flute. Arrow Keeper already totters on his own grave. Once he crosses over, you will make no more he-bear talk. If you do, perhaps Medicine Flute will hint to his worshipers

47

that an enemy within us must be executed."

"Buck, are you chewing peyote? Why do you make speeches and taunt me now while our enemy escapes with our—"

And then, reading the mocking glint in Wolf Who Hunts Smiling's eyes, Touch the Sky finally understood.

"You traitor," he breathed softly. For a moment he recalled his brave Apache friend Victorio Grayeyes, who had watched Mexican soldiers slaughter his entire family after a turncoat uncle led them to their hidden cave. "You treacherous, low-crawling, double-tongued dog! You have just shed the blood of your own and helped our enemy steal our ponies!"

"See? Once again, just like a woman, you show your feelings in your face."

"I do, and this time with no shame! This crime defies a stoic. A warrior with a heart has to show his hatred when a Cheyenne helps Comanches butcher fellow Cheyennes."

By now the braves who had kept their ponies in camp were pounding closer, the war cry sounding.

"It is my word against yours, White Man Runs Him," Wolf Who Hunts Smiling said. "And after Medicine Flute's great miracle this night, your word is worth less than a spent cartridge!"

Chapter Four

The lightning raid by the Comanche shifted attention away from Medicine Flute's apparent miracle. An official council of all the adult males was called on the morning following the tragedy of the stolen herd and murdered guards.

But in truth, informal councils had been held all night, warriors remaining vigilant and meeting with their clan or soldier troops to discuss this new emergency. Although some ponies had been safe in camp, all of the well-rested animals had been among the grazing herd. Some braves had tried to follow on tired mounts. But they were quickly left behind. Only River of Winds, the best scout in camp, was ordered to keep trailing them.

Almost every clan had lost ponies, some braves losing every pony on their string. And throughout the night, everyone heard the keening wails of the wives, mothers, and sisters mourning the four brutally slain guards.

While listening to the cries, Touch the Sky agonized. How should he handle this new and dangerous situation with Wolf Who Hunts Smiling? Once again the tall young warrior had no witnesses to confirm the other brave's treachery. In fact, he himself had no proof that could be picked up and examined. Yet, he knew the truth deep in his innermost core.

Before reporting to the council lodge, Touch the Sky cut short his hair to mourn their new dead, as was the custom. Then he joined Tangle Hair and Little Horse and filed into the hide-covered council lodge. Arrow Keeper, Chief Gray Thunder, and the clan headmen occupied one side of the huge lodge; the other was quickly filled with braves who counted 16 winters or more.

A clay pipe was stuffed with a mixture of rich tobacco and fragrant red-willow bark. When all who wished to had smoked the common pipe, Chief Gray Thunder laid it down between his leg and Arrow Keeper's, signaling the beginning of discussion.

"Brothers!" Gray Thunder said. "All you who are gathered here now know what has happened. Who could not? We are now pony warriors without ponies! We must discuss our battle plan. We must quickly make plans to acquire a few more ponies immediately.

"Once again, Cheyennes, we have cut short our hair because of Comanche treachery. First they took our women and children, now they have our ponies. Our women and children are back with us now"—here Gray Thunder recognized Touch the Sky with a nod in his direction—"thanks to the bravery and skill of our warriors. What Cheyennes have done, Cheyennes will do! Once again our ponies will graze the lush grass of the Powder River country."

Gray Thunder was still a vigorous warrior despite having some 40 winters behind him. Only now were the first streaks of silver showing in his hair.

"Black Elk," he said, "you are our battle chief. How do you counsel?"

"Father, these drunken thieves from the south country are as wily as any Pawnees. This raid, it could well be an elaborate ruse to lure all the warriors from camp so our enemy might capture the women and children. We made this mistake once before. I say, never again!

"First, we must quickly visit True Bow's Lakota village at Elbow Bend. They will give us more ponies. Then, a small but deadly band chosen from our best warriors must ride south under the raised hatchet."

Black Elk frowned as some memory returned.

"This Big Tree, the one who ties a roadrunner skin to the tail of his pony. When did Black Elk ever hide behind his tipi? Yet, I freely admit I have never seen a more dangerous foe! Once, near Blanco Canyon, several of us thought we had trapped him. We were fools! Fathers and brothers, he sat backward on his pony while

51

it galloped. He held a great fistful of arrows and fired them so rapidly that he emptied two quivers in the time it takes a hungry man to eat a handful of cherries."

Gray Thunder nodded. A quick voice vote of the headmen approved Black Elk's plan. Among those selected to ride out were Black Elk, Wolf Who Hunts Smiling, Little Horse, and Touch the Sky. Because his own coup feathers reached nearly to the ground, Gray Thunder was not voted down when he insisted on riding with the war party.

When this business was completed, Wolf Who Hunts Smiling rose to his feet.

"Fathers and brothers! Hear me! The raid this past night naturally has the thoughts of all red-blooded warriors set toward revenge against the cricket-eating marauders. But let us not forget what may, after all, have been the most important event of all."

The Cheyenne paused and carefully stepped around his brothers, making his way to the back wall. He took up a place beside Medicine Flute. This brave sat cross-legged, his leg-bone flute lying across his lap.

"You have, all of you, eyes to see. Who can deny that Medicine Flute set a star on fire, then sent it flaming across the sky?"

"He did," someone said.

"I saw it," another said.

"All of us did!"

"At first glance," Arrow Keeper said quietly, not bothering to stand as the younger men did, "what appears to be an elk may turn out to be a

Cheyenne dressed in buckskins. What we see is not always what we shoot at. Appearances are seldom reliable."

At these words the lodge went stone still and silent. All eyes turned toward Black Elk. By now all had heard the story about how Black Elk had once fired at Touch the Sky, supposedly mistaking his buckskins for an elk's hide.

"Elks?" Wolf Who Hunts Smiling injected a condescending tone into his voice, as if he were indulging a slow-witted child. "Old Grandfather, no one is speaking of elks. But of course, the power of Medicine Flute's magic has understandably rattled you. And do not forget, Medicine Flute described this event before it passed. But of course, at your advanced age, many things are easily forgotten."

This was the first time Wolf Who Hunts Smiling had ever called the shaman grandfather instead of father, and Arrow Keeper had noticed it.

"Truly," he said, "I have forgotten more than you will ever learn. And still I am the wiser."

"As you say, Grandfather." Wolf Who Hunts Smiling winked for the benefit of some of his Bull Whip brothers in the last row. "But what I wish to say is this. We will need strong medicine to achieve success on this mission. Therefore, I say Medicine Flute should ride out, too!"

"You will have strong medicine," Arrow Keeper said quietly. "The strongest. For Touch the Sky is riding with you."

"We will have a stout fighter in Touch the Sky," Wolf Who Hunts Smiling said. "That much no man disputes. But who, besides Arrow Keeper or Little Horse, claims to have truly witnessed any magic? Yes, yes, we all know the story from Shoots Left Handed's band up north in the Bear Paw Mountains. How Touch the Sky supposedly turned bluecoat bullets to sand. But why is it that we ourselves have never seen the miracles?

"In contrast, Cheyennes, only think on what Medicine Flute did in front of the entire tribe, as he predicted. I say, let him ride with us!"

This brought a loud chorus of support, and Touch the Sky realized that the moment he'd been waiting for had come. He rose to his feet.

"I am going to kill Wolf Who Hunts Smiling."

His announcement struck everyone dumb, including Wolf Who Hunts Smiling and the Bull Whips. Little Horse gaped; even Arrow Keeper looked dumbfounded.

"You heard me straight," he went on. "His scaffold is as good as built. I will kill this murderer of Cheyennes, this traitor to his own tribe."

Gray Thunder frowned, the furrow between his eyebrows deepening. "Buck, I have long been weary of the feud between you and Wolf Who Hunts Smiling. These are strong words. Both this talk of murdering Cheyennes and this talk of traitors."

"Yes, they are strong words, Father, for they must match the crimes. I do not speak them lightly."

"Why speak them at all?"

"Because, Father, they are true words and truth should be uncovered." Touch the Sky made the cutoff sign. "You all knew Born in Snow. He was no warrior to be taken by surprise. Every one of the murdered Bow String guards was an honor to Spotted Tail's troop! Count upon it, Big Tree did not steal our ponies or kill our herd guards without valuable help. Help from one inside our own tribe."

Arrow Keeper and Little Horse knew, better than any other brave present, that Touch the Sky never gave the name of truth to any statement unless it flew straight arrow.

"What proof do you have?" Gray Thunder demanded.

Touch the Sky shook his head. "Nothing I can place in your sash. But I swear by the four directions this one conspired with Big Tree. If he did not actually draw the blood of our dead companions, he at least allowed it to flow."

By now Wolf Who Hunts Smiling realized Touch the Sky had no more surprises to spring. He again flashed his furtive smile, dark eyes mocking the taller Cheyenne.

"He is driven by desperation. This is choice jesting indeed, this business of accusing others in the tribe of being spies. This one drank whiskey with the same murdering whites who killed our people! Now Medicine Flute has exposed his magic for what it truly is, a thing of smoke, and he attempts to turn me into a traitor to disguise his own treachery."

This set the lodge buzzing. Gray Thunder

frowned again and folded his arms, the signal for silence.

"A good chief does not dictate to the people. But, brothers, this is no time for a clash of ambitious young bulls! We must paint our faces and make ready our battle rigs. The tribe must come together as one to retrieve our pony herd. The others want him, so Medicine Flute will ride with us. The tribe has spoken with one voice."

No one disputed this. Now Chief Gray Thunder met Touch the Sky's eyes.

"I will brook no more talk of traitors and killing our own. Is this thing clear?"

Touch the Sky nodded once. He saw Medicine Flute and Wolf Who Hunts Smiling exchange a triumphant glance. Again Touch the Sky recalled his dead companions lying mutilated on the ground and recalled that glint in Wolf Who Hunts Smiling's eyes and his taunting words: *It is my word against yours, White Man Runs Him.*

"As you say, Gray Thunder," he finally replied. "No more talking."

By the time the council ended, rain clouds had blown in from the Bighorn Mountains. Touch the Sky was among the first to exit the lodge. His thoughts were skittering around inside his skull like frenzied rodents. Right then he did not feel like facing any of his friends and explaining his bold words in council.

He hurried across camp and untethered his bay. She nuzzled his shoulder, glad to see him.

He would have to prepare his battle rig since the war party would ride out soon. But for now the confused thoughts warring inside him made him desire solitude.

He knew a peaceful spot downriver from camp where, toward sunset, the young, unmarried bucks sometimes held the girls of their choice in their blankets for love talk. It was a sheltered glade, lush with lavender, vines of blue morning glory, and wild orchids. During the day it was almost always deserted. Several times he had visited the spot when, following Arrow Keeper's advice, he wished to stop all thought and simply listen to the language of his senses.

Thunder muttered in the distance, and dark clouds obscured the high rimland to the west. He slipped the hide headstall on his pony and rode out. He looked neither right or left.

During a brief ride along the grassy riverbank, he watched the cottonwood leaves turn their undersides out, a prelude to the coming storm. He reached the glade and left his bay on a long tether in the lush grass. He stepped past a wall of hawthorn bushes and immediately felt the presence of another person.

Thinking of the Comanche raiders, his hand went to the beaded sheath of his knife.

"No enemy here, Cheyenne warrior. So the council is over? But I am so glad to finally see you!"

Although it startled him, Honey Eater's voice also tugged his lips into a smile. A heartbeat later he spotted her. She sat in the shelter of a weeping willow. The low-hanging branches formed a soft green curtain around her.

"Yes, it is over, little one. And soon Black Elk will be raging throughout camp, searching for you. I should leave, or you had best return."

He was right, but neither of them moved. The wind whipped up, fluttering the leaves. Muttering thunder gathered into a sudden clap that made Honey Eater wince.

He moved closer, parted the willow branches, and knelt beside her. She was fragrant from the fresh white columbine petals braided into her hair. A soft doeskin dress molded itself to the delicate curves and hollows of her body.

Normally, on the rare occasions when they met alone like this, they could not help touching and embracing. But lately there was a curious tension between them, and they avoided such closeness. Touch the Sky knew why. It had not been so very long since Honey Eater, whose simple heart was guileless, had frankly told him that in her heart she was his wife. And if he sent for her, then somehow, some way, she would lie with him as his woman.

Touch the Sky wanted her with a passion that sang in his blood. But asking her to meet him like an animal in the forest and exposing her further to Black Elk's jealous, murderous wrath—that and the strict Cheyenne taboo against adultery gave him pause. It was as if they both sensed that one touch between them could lead to a storm of dangerous passion.

But now she clearly had something more urgent on her mind—something she had been impatient to tell him.

"Touch the Sky! Two Twists told me you sometimes come here. I have been coming to this place each day, hoping to see you. You are no stranger to unfair suffering. But this time you are up against it! Wolf Who Hunts Smiling and his Bull Whip brothers are determined this time to either kill you or destroy you."

Quickly, she told him what she had overheard when the Whips had met behind Black Elk's tipi and planned the ruse with the comet.

"Black Elk is in it, too, of course," she said bitterly. "But now I clearly understand a thing. Black Elk is mixed up in his cousin's schemes only to get at you. Jealousy long ago destroyed his sense of fairness. He is only a dangerous pawn.

"But Wolf Who Hunts Smiling, he is surely the Red Man's devil! I see now that he is driven by the base impulse for power. Nothing, not the thought of the Arrows nor the welfare of his tribe, will come between him and his brutal ambition. And this Medicine Flute, he is well suited to such treachery!"

"Clearly you know both of them well," Touch the Sky said, nodding. "Wolf Who Hunts Smiling missed his opportunity to kill me when he might have. Now he does the next best thing by giving the lie to my medicine—and thus Arrow Keeper's."

Honey Eater glanced around them at this peaceful spot where the purling of the river and the soft warbling of the thrush so often lulled couples in love. A huge crystal tear formed on her eyelid and zigzagged down her cheek.

"My father was right," she said bitterly. "Happiness is a short, warm moment; suffering is a long, cold night."

Another rolling crash of thunder. A far-flung spider web of lightning electrified the sky.

"How much must you suffer, brave Cheyenne warrior? How much? Enemies outside, enemies inside. Is there no end to this hating and killing and base plotting? On the night you first vowed your love for me, when we were both trapped in the whiskey traders' camp, even as you spoke your love, they were torturing you!

"Look around us now. This place where happiness normally reigns. You, too, should be strolling down here nights to meet a pretty maiden. Where is your life, your happiness?"

"Here I sit," Touch the Sky replied, "beside the prettiest girl in our tribe. And the only one I love. You are my life and my happiness, and I desire no other."

Another tear chased the first down her cheek. "And you are mine, Touch the Sky. But how can I be as cruel as your enemies and deny you your life?"

He shook his head, banishing all such talk forever. "Know this, little Honey Eater. I would rather have you this tortured and painful way than any other woman I might have freely."

"My father—" She hesitated. But he touched her hand, encouraging her to give word shapes to the feelings troubling her. Now soft tendrils of rain lashed at their faces.

"My father, just before he crossed over, he rose up from his deathbed and spoke startling things to me. One thing he said was that you were meant to be a great chief. He told me, 'Love him, my little daughter, but know that his way will be hard.'"

She looked long and hard into Touch the Sky's eyes. "I must go. You are right. Black Elk will scour camp for me, and we are both at risk. But first, tell me a thing. Do you believe there is a destiny already in the stars for us? Touch the Sky, will we ever live openly as husband and wife? Will we have a child? None of these things did my father tell me."

His pulse throbbed in his palms, and cool sweat broke out on his back. For these questions were the very same ones that often plagued the peace of his sleeping hours. They rose and, hand in hand, walked slowly to the edge of the glade.

He said, "Arrow Keeper's teachings have indeed convinced me that every human destiny is already written in the stars. However, even Arrow Keeper has no magic to tell exactly what that destiny will be."

"The song the young girls sing in their sewing lodge," she said timidly. "It is about us. And according to the song, we will be married and have a child."

He nodded. "I have heard it." Indeed, hearing that very song had stopped him once when, discovering that Black Elk had whipped Honey Eater, he had been on the verge of killing his rival. Such violence would have banished him forever from the tribe and, thus, Honey Eater.

"But now you ride out again," Honey Eater

said. "And this time, you face the loathsome Big Tree. His very glance makes my skin crawl! He is a sick Indian, crazy in his eyes. As if he were not danger enough, Black Elk, Wolf Who Hunts Smiling, and other tribal enemies will surround you during this mission. Touch the Sky, I am frightened like never before. May the Holy Ones ride with you!"

With that she rose quickly on tiptoe and did what Indians seldom did—she kissed him. A moment later she was gone, leaving Touch the Sky alone with his aching heart and troubling thoughts.

Chapter Five

Big Tree and his Comanche warriors drove their stolen pony herd hard to the southwest, stopping only to graze them in the lush grass near the rivers.

These ponies, like all wild stock, were much sturdier and better able to survive harsh conditions than the coddled, overbred horses ridden by white men. Paleface horses were bigger and clumsier, spoiled by diets of good grain and forage. Indian ponies, in contrast, could survive a hard winter by nibbling on cottonwood bark and twigs and stunted brown grass trapped under the snow.

Mustangs were also used to covering great distances at a run. With the braves riding at the fringe of the herd, the Comanches set a grueling pace. Their riding skills were second to none on the plains. The braves seemed mere extensions of their horses, bouncing along on top of them with seemingly effortless ease. A Comanche could ride without holding on, freeing his hands to load and fire weapons. Indeed, many of the braves, copying their leader, wore two quivers to accommodate all the arrows they could launch in a short time.

Big Tree knew the Cheyennes would eventually follow them. They could trade with neighboring tribes for a few replacement ponies. But it would require the rest of the warm moons to again track and capture so many magnificent animals. Besides, no Plains Indian tribe would abide such a strike without revenge. Not to avenge it was as good as an invitation to terrorize their homeland yet again.

Yes, the Cheyennes would eventually follow them south. And once the Comanches reached the dry plains of Southern Colorado, the pace would become much slower as the rivers—and thus, the grass—grew more sparse. Then the Cheyennes might catch up to them.

Big Tree circled the herd and selected the brave named Stone Club.

"Ride our back trail," he told him. "Wolf Who Hunts Smiling will soon be sending a word-bringer ahead to us. Relay the message back to me."

Stone Club filled his parfleche with parched corn, then pointed his pony toward the north again. After the brave's departure, Big Tree found himself smiling again. This Wolf Who Hunts Smiling—what sort of treachery against his own tribe was he planning? Clearly, this renegade Cheyenne hated the tall shaman nearly as much as Big Tree himself. Perhaps even more, if such were possible.

Again Big Tree thought of the honey-skinned maiden who had driven the leaders Iron Eyes and Hairy Wolf giddy with loin heat. How cleverly she had brought about their downfall by driving a wedge between them. Big Tree had vowed to top her himself—perhaps someday he would make good on his vow. After all, Wolf Who Hunts Smiling had vowed they would share the fruits of power.

But for now, one thing at a time. Soon his wily Cheyenne ally would send word of the next move to destroy this haughty shaman.

"Brothers," the Lakota chief named True Bow said. "We knew these Comanche dogs were riding north. But our scouts were sure it was a raiding party aimed at the hair-face settlements. We Lakota drove them out once, and they fear us. For unlike them, a Sioux warrior is not afraid to die!"

True Bow paused and took stock of his Cheyenne visitors. The two groups looked distinct in the clear, early morning light of the Sioux camp. True Bow and his braves wore their hair long, tightly braided, and wrapped around their heads. Their Cheyenne cousins, in contrast, wore their hair roughly cropped short in honor of their slain companions.

"True it is," True Bow said, "that I signed the hair-face talking paper. I have pledged this Lakota band to peace with all red men and white men alike. I have pledged neither to raise my battle-ax nor assist those who do."

The old chief fell silent, thinking. The Lakota Sioux and the Cheyennes had fought as one people from their earliest days on the plains, even intermarrying with little fuss. Now they spoke in the easy mix of Sioux and Cheyenne words understood by both tribes. His Cheyenne visitors included Touch the Sky, Little Horse, Black Elk, and Wolf Who Hunts Smiling and his new companion, Medicine Flute. All stood a respectful few paces behind Chief Gray Thunder.

"I respect your pledge," Gray Thunder said. "You do not keep it out of cowardice. Your camp includes the best warriors on the northern plains. And I was there at Hanging Woman Creek, True Bow, fighting in my first battle, when you led combined Sioux and Cheyenne warriors against Roaring Bear's Utes."

True Bow's face divided in a wide smile. "The fish eaters!" he said with contempt. "Well, buck, did we give those big, lumbering fools a war face? Now it is said the Ute are a mountain tribe. You young bucks, pin my words to your sash. They live in the mountains only because Sioux and Cheyennes drove them there!"

"I have ears for this," Black Elk said, and his younger cousin nodded, too.

Again True Bow fell silent. He gazed out

across the neat clan circles. Sioux tipis were taller and more narrow than those of their cousins, with no hide flap over the entrance. The Sioux were not nearly so modest as Cheyennes, and couples often made love in public.

But True Bow was gazing at the wild mustangs gathered in a buffalo-rope corral near the river.

"True, I have pledged not to assist any war party. But this here today, it is not strictly war. You are a horse tribe. These insect eaters from the desert, they have taken the very lifeblood of your people. It is a question of getting back what is rightly yours."

The old chief's brow was furrowed with age and worry. Now he hunched his shoulders under his blanket and said, "Take what you need, brothers. You can pay us back from your own herd when you recover them. Had I not pledged my people to the peace road, our lances would be raised beside yours."

"With your good ponies," Black Elk said confidently, "we will be enough to do the hurt dance on them."

But Touch the Sky and Little Horse were watching Wolf Who Hunts Smiling. The wily young brave exchanged a long glance with Medicine Flute. Both braves traded a knowing half smile.

Medicine Flute saw Touch the Sky watching. He raised his leg-bone flute by way of mocking salute.

* * *

The Sioux ponies were wild mustangs not yet broken to human riders. They had been driven into captivity with plans to divide and break them later.

Each man in the Cheyenne war party was permitted to select one pony, giving each a remount for the long chase. Touch the Sky rode the perimeter of the corral until he spotted the pony he wanted: a pure white mare with a silky gray mane.

Little Horse, flicking a light sisal whip to control his pony, was moving to cut out a claybank he liked. The other braves, too, had made their selections.

It was in their differing styles of breaking green horses that Touch the Sky had truly learned the vast differences between the white man and the red man. The white man, consistent with his belief in ownership of land and animals and even people, deliberately broke a horse's wild spirit and dominated it. The red man, in contrast, saw his pony as an equal companion in the struggle for survival. And the animal's wild nature must be respected in order to gain the survival edge.

White men began by beating, blindfolding, and starving a horse. They shoved iron in the animals' mouths, nailed iron to their hooves, and strapped cumbersome saddles and headstalls to them.

Red men, in contrast, simply jumped on and rode the horse. If the Indian was still clinging

to the pony when it finally quit running, it
was his.

The mare veered out of his way when Touch
the Sky nudged his mount closer. He tugged
his hackamore right and circled again, trap-
ping the mare between him and the buffalo-
hair ropes. The bay surged closer, and Touch
the Sky leaped.

He landed on the mare solidly enough and
caught a good grip on her mane. But with a
suddenness that shocked him, she hopped vio-
lently to the right, then bucked hard. A heartbeat later he was flying through the air. He
landed hard in the deep grass and had to look
sharp to avoid being trampled.

"Woman Face shows his surprise!" Wolf Who
Hunts Smiling taunted him.

Touch the Sky ignored him, rising to his feet.
This time he didn't even bother with his bay.
His mouth a grim, determined slit, he simply
charged the white mare.

She saw him coming and fled. But he had
guessed her direction of flight. Now he leaped
that way as she moved, landing hard on her
back and wrapping his arms about her well-
muscled neck to hang on.

Several Sioux observers whistled and
shouted, untying one of the ropes. The
white mare tore out across the short-grass
plain. Touch the Sky hung on for dear life,
bouncing from side to side, always on the
feather edge of being tossed clear.

On and on the sturdy little mustang raced,
infuriated by this human beast clinging to her.

Touch the Sky could hear Little Horse and the others all around him, likewise pitting their wills against the animals' struggles. Occasionally the pony would suddenly halt and hop, bucking hard and trying to shake him again. But Touch the Sky clung tightly despite the battering to his ribs and groin.

Sister Sun was well through her journey across the sky when the pony and Touch the Sky, both bone weary, returned to the Sioux village at Elbow Bend.

"She is yours, brother!" Little Horse greeted him triumphantly. His own claybank now grazed quietly, submitting as Little Horse scratched her withers.

Touch the Sky nodded. The ponies would still have to be halter broken. But since Indian headstalls included no iron bits, the ponies would not rebel so severely as mounts broken by hair faces.

Time was critical, so the Cheyennes moved out that same day. It was no problem to cut sign on the Comanches—not when they were driving an entire pony herd before them.

"Our enemy travels by night, too," Touch the Sky told Little Horse. "See all the rocks turned over? Rocks they would have avoided by day."

Little Horse nodded. Earlier, they had gone through the painstaking process of estimating how many Comanches they were trailing. This was done by starting at the very edge of the tracks to sort out the individual riders. The depth of the print separated mounted horses from mustangs.

They counted some 20 riders. "Twice that number," Little Horse said, "if you count Big Tree's true battle worth."

And through all of it, whether riding or snatching a quick rest before resuming the grueling trek, Medicine Flute quietly mocked Touch the Sky.

Knowing they were safe from their fleeing enemies that first night, the Cheyennes made a meat camp with a cooking fire. Earlier Little Horse had shot an antelope near the Trinidad River. They butchered out the hindquarters and roasted them over blazing driftwood.

After the meal, when sentries had been posted and the braves had rolled into their buffalo robes for the night, the eerie flute music began.

"Brother," Little Horse said in a low voice beside Touch the Sky, "count upon it. This journey is not merely to regain our ponies from the Comanche. Your enemies within the tribe also plan to challenge your shaman powers. So far they cannot kill your body. So now they plan to lay your powerful spirit to rest."

"Straight words, brother, though I am not so sure as you just how powerful my spirit is."

"Deeds speak louder than words, tall buck. Did I not stand beside you, unarmed, while an entire unit of bluecoat soldiers shot at us from less than a stone's throw away? And did one bullet hit us? To me, this is power and nothing else. You have strong medicine."

Touch the Sky lay on his back, watching countless stars glitter in the black dome overhead. He heard the horses snuffling, frogs croaking, cicadas sounding their monotonous rhythm. Arrow Keeper's words drifted back to him from the hinterland of memory: *For every war path, there is a spirit path.*

But always mocking him, challenging him, setting his nerves on raw edge—the dull, monotonous notes of Medicine Flute's hollowed-out leg-bone flute.

Chapter Six

The Cheyenne war party rode hard throughout the next day, stopping only to water their mounts. They ate on horseback, subsisting on the pemmican and jerked buffalo in their legging sashes. They switched often to their new remounts and used this opportunity to learn the ponies' personalities, their individual strengths and weaknesses.

Touch the Sky's new mare showed ideal traits for a warrior's pony: inexhaustible stamina, reckless courage, surefooted agility. The Cheyenne learned how to sense, with his knees and thighs, the mare's subtle muscular contractions that signaled a jump or turn; in turn, the mustang learned to sense the precise meaning of Touch the Sky's nudges and tugs.

All day long Wolf Who Hunts Smiling and Medicine Flute mocked Touch the Sky with their eyes. Meantime, their Comanche enemies' path did not alter: a bead-straight line toward the dusty canyons, arroyos, and mesas of their arid Southwestern homeland.

River of Winds, the only Cheyenne sent to trail the Comanches on the night of the raid, had not yet returned with a report. But the Cheyennes—despite many personal differences—agreed to the last man on one point: If the Comanches reached their beloved Blanco Canyon, the herd was lost. Not even heavily armed bluecoats dared attack this Comanche stronghold.

Touch the Sky knew the Blanco well—the way a survivor knows a horrible disease. True, he and a small band had managed to infiltrate the canyon. But once within, they were fortunate to have escaped with their lives, let alone mounted an attack. The canyon could not even be approached safely. It was stuck in the middle of the notorious *Llano Estacado* or Staked Plain, where the only ground cover consisted of the bones of dehydrated men and animals.

No, the Comanches must be caught even before they reached the Texas Panhandle and New Mexico Territory. The fight would be hard enough, even if they were caught. But Touch the Sky and Little Horse both realized something else. Wolf Who Hunts Smiling's new plan represented as serious a threat as any official enemy of the Cheyenne.

74

That night they camped in a sheltered canyon lined with traprock shelves.

"Brother," Little Horse said quietly when the two friends had separated themselves from the others. He made the cutoff sign. "I cannot stop seeing the dead faces of Born in Snow and the other guards. You have said Wolf Who Hunts Smiling had a hand in their deaths. Since you said it, I believe it. But I confess, though there is little I thought him incapable of doing, never did I expect him to nail his colors to a Comanche lodgepole. He has sullied our Arrows!"

Touch the Sky nodded, his mouth held in a grim, determined slit. "He has, buck. They are dripping blood even now."

"And listen. There it is again. Medicine Flute and his eternal tune. I have always wondered if a buzzard can vomit. I shall find out if one hears this music. They are goading us, buck, and I confess, since Wolf Who Hunts Smiling's treachery a few sleeps ago, I am keen to meet them."

Touch the Sky shook his head. "Do not rise to their bait. Only keep your eyes and ears sharp, stout buck. Even now Wolf Who Hunts Smiling and his shaman have their heads bent together. Count upon it, another monster is being bred."

"Do it this night," Wolf Who Hunts Smiling told his new medicine man. "You know what to say. Earlier today, when I rode out to scout our flanks, I met with the Comanche word-bringer Stone Club. Now they have their instructions.

All will be ready when we arrive. Then White Man Runs Him will feel heat in his face."

Medicine Flute only smiled his heavy-lidded smile, nodding slightly. He didn't miss a note of his eerie fluting.

"This music," Wolf Who Hunts Smiling said. "It would make the Wendigo himself tear out his hair. Gray Thunder is on the verge of ordering a halt to your playing. But play on, play on, buck. Woman Face and Little Horse hate it more than I do."

Wolf Who Hunts Smiling studied the shadows and decided the time was right. He rose and strode to the middle of camp.

"Chief Gray Thunder! Brothers! Have ears for my words."

"Now the snake drives home his fangs," Little Horse told Touch the Sky.

"I have a sporting challenge," Wolf Who Hunts Smiling said. "A friendly challenge. We have two shamen with us. I do not believe both of them can possess the true shaman's eye. Therefore, I ask this thing in the name of the tribe. Give the rest of us proof one of you has the true shaman's eye."

"A friendly challenge from you," Little Horse said, "is no better than a bullet from a bluecoat rifle. This is more treachery."

"Of course, speak up for your master. White men run him, and he runs you."

"Your mouth is like the back end of a horse," Touch the Sky said, "and produces the same thing."

"You two," Gray Thunder said, "still fighting between yourselves even as we pursue an enemy. Why not just join them and fight on their side against us?"

"Yes," Touch the Sky said, his eyes boring into Wolf Who Hunts Smiling's. "Why not just join them, indeed? You are as good as on their side now."

"Of course you ignore my challenge and try to veer the talk onto me. For Medicine Flute stands ready to expose your deceit! Just as you are a pretend Cheyenne, so are you a pretend shaman. If you truly have strong medicine, why fear my challenge?"

Touch the Sky ached to expose the recent treachery involving the comet. But to do so would put Honey Eater at great risk.

"You are a fool, Panther Clan. Do you think the Great Medicine Man gave magic to mortals for frivolous sport? To perform tricks on command, like trained ponies?"

Black Elk joined his cousin in the fray. "This is not frivolous sport! We are up against a powerful foe. My cousin speaks straight; our tribe's medicine has grown weak. This challenge my cousin proposes, it may help us decide which brave truly has medicine. All of us saw Medicine Flute send a burning star across the heavens! No wonder Touch the Sky is reluctant to lock horns with such a powerful bull!"

Touch the Sky felt the noose tightening again as he realized that his refusal to demean the magic taught to him by Arrow Keeper would be held as a confession that he was a pretend shaman.

"This gets out of hand," Gray Thunder said. "I am no shaman. Never have I experienced a vision. But Touch the Sky spoke right. Matters of the spirit are not meant for such a show."

Many sitting in a circle around the fire nodded agreement.

"I always have ears for our chief," Wolf Who Hunts Smiling said. "But my cousin speaks straight. We are on an important mission. Never mind my suggestion for a challenge. Is it not fair to ask at least this of our two shamen. Has either one sensed or felt anything since we rode out? A sign about this mission?"

This struck the listeners as reasonable. Many nodded, including Gray Thunder. As if on signal, all stared at Touch the Sky.

After a long silence, listening to wind whistle through the nearby canyon walls, Touch the Sky shook his head. "I have experienced nothing."

Now everyone turned to look at Medicine Flute. Unperturbed, the slender youth laid his leg-bone flute across one knee. "Certainly I have seen things, though still the reason for seeing them is not clear. Sometimes we must wait for the wind to abate before we can see patterns in the snow."

"What things have you seen?" Wolf Who Hunts Smiling encouraged him.

"Things not meant for the faint of heart, buck! Visions that portend a great sadness. I saw a Cheyenne pony, screaming in pain as it floated on a river of blood. I saw a charred circle within a vast clearing, I saw bloody entrails, and I saw a rack of charred rib bones protruding from the ground."

A long silence greeted these disturbing, mysterious words. Little Horse glanced at Touch the Sky, but the taller Cheyenne only shrugged helplessly. He could not fake a vision simply to rival this so-called shaman.

The silence was finally broken when Medicine Flute raised his leg-bone instrument to his lips and began piping his eerie notes.

River of Winds rode a fresh mount and was unencumbered by heavy equipment. He caught up with Big Tree's Comanches just north of the white soldiertown called Fort Pueblo. This was Southern Colorado plains country, semiarid and hilly, with plenty of buttes and redrock canyons to offer shelter.

The canyons and blind cliffs kept the Comanches vigilant as they guided their stolen herd. Carefully avoiding their outlying flank riders, River of Winds managed to ride within hailing distance of the herd. He was well hidden behind the rimrock when the Comanches grouped the herd for the night in a grassy draw near a stream.

As dark descended, River of Winds moved in closer. Carefully he picked his way over a talus slide, fearful of dislodging a rock. The noise of a rider approaching from the north sent him quickly to the ground. He watched Big Tree confer for some time with the scout he had sent out earlier to cover their back trail.

River of Winds knew that his tribe would have sent out a war party by now. No doubt this scout had ridden back to check on their progress. Whatever it was he reported, it made the fearsome Big Tree grin like a skull.

Big Tree barked out a command and two of his braves, carrying braided horsehair ropes and a hackamore, crossed toward the grazing pony herd. They cut out a magnificent ginger stallion, leading it by the hackamore and bringing it back to camp.

It was a fine pony, one River of Winds had admired when Tangle Hair claimed it and put his clan mark on it. Perhaps Big Tree was selecting it for his own string.

The Cheyenne watched Big Tree admire the fine animal. He scratched its withers and stroked the finely muscled flanks. He nodded several times, praising the pony.

River of Winds felt his face flush with apprehension when Big Tree slid the Colt pistol from his sash.

Big Tree set the hammer at half cock and spun the cylinder, inspecting the load. A heartbeat later he lifted the weapon and planted a slug in the pony's brain.

River of Winds winced as an arc of blood shot out and the pony's knees buckled like sticks snapping. Casually, Big Tree set his pistol at half cock again and cleared out the spent cap. He reloaded the cylinder.

To a Cheyenne, ponies were almost as human as his fellow Indians. So River of Winds was forced to choke back retches of nausea as he witnessed the rest of it.

While the cactus-liquor *pulque* flowed freely, the drunken Comanches butchered the pony. Its coiled entrails were pulled through slits and roasted in the hot embers. Meaty steaks were cut from the haunches. The skull was cracked open with rocks and the brains roasted, then mixed with a soup made from the blood and organs.

A huge fire was built in the center of the camp clearing. Remembering his instructions from Wolf Who Hunts Smiling, Big Tree directed that the pony's ribs be set up on end as a cooking rack for the steaks. Far into the night, the Comanches feasted on the Cheyenne pony.

But River of Winds felt his smoldering rage nearly give way to helpless tears when five more ponies were shot. These were not eaten. But each was savagely gutted, its entrails spread in greasy heaps for the Cheyenne pursuers to discover.

Chapter Seven

"Only look! You have eyes to see. It is just as Medicine Flute described it!"

Wolf Who Hunts Smiling's voice was smug with triumph. He sat his paint at the head of the long, grassy draw where their enemy had camped. The scene, as they rode upon it late in the afternoon, had shocked them to the core of their souls: the pony guts strewn everywhere, even dangling from tree limbs; the hollowed-out, decapitated carcasses and the heads left on stakes; the gnawed bones left over from this barbaric feast.

And reigning in the middle of this macabre tableau was the blackened-ribs cooking rack, rising from the ground just as Medicine Flute had described it.

"They are eating our ponies!" Tangle Hair

said bitterly. "Though game is plentiful. And look how many were slaughtered for no reason."

"There is a reason," Black Elk said. "They do this thing to taunt us. They know that no tribe on the plains respects ponies more than we. But they make one mistake. Such as this does not make true men wring their hands in fear. It only goads them to a war cry."

Wolf Who Hunts Smiling aimed a sly glance at Touch the Sky. "It is grisly. But at least we know we finally have a shaman whose medicine is powerful indeed."

Touch the Sky rode out ahead, then turned his pony to address Wolf Who Hunts Smiling and the rest of the group.

"We know nothing, Panther Clan. Our tribe has an official shaman already. His name is Arrow Keeper, and his medicine is respected throughout the red nations. The Council of Forty decides who our medicine man will be, not a power-starved Bull Whip who speaks from both sides of his mouth."

"I have no ears for this, Woman Face! Our own chief has witnessed this thing. You were trained by Arrow Keeper. Yet do you deny that you could see nothing, while Medicine Flute told us a vision that came true?"

"True, I saw nothing because Maiyun chose not to reveal it. And, yes, I do deny that Medicine Flute had a vision."

"You fool!" Wolf Who Hunt Smiling glanced from Chief Gray Thunder to Black Elk. "Here is the scene, just as Medicine Flute foretold.

How else could this thing be, if not ordained by a vision?"

Touch the Sky felt a tight bubble of helpless rage swelling inside his chest. This thing was awkward. Even Little Horse was clearly impressed by the apparent vision.

"How else could it be? Simple, low-crawling wolf. You have conspired with our enemies! You had a bloody hand in the death of our guards, and you now play the fox with Big Tree against us."

This charge struck most of those present as preposterous. True, all knew that Wolf Who Hunts Smiling was ambitious. All knew, too, that he hated this Touch the Sky with a belligerent passion. But to play the turncoat against his own tribe and with such an enemy as this?

It was a serious charge. Long had Wolf Who Hunts Smiling and others likewise accused Touch the Sky of being a spy for the palefaces. But they did not level specific charges for specific crimes, as Touch the Sky was doing now.

It was Gray Thunder who spoke.

"Touch the Sky, you are a warrior unlikely to die in his sleep. I was told how you stood shoulder to shoulder with Little Horse and fought off the white hunters at the Buffalo Battle. And never will I forget the time when you rallied the junior warriors and saved our women and children from Comanche and Kiowas. Unlike some in the tribe, I no longer question your loyalty to your people.

"But, buck, these are serious words you speak against Wolf Who Hunts Smiling. You call him a traitor, an offense which, if proven, means sure death. Twice now have you said this thing. All right then, Cheyenne. Where is your proof—proof I can pick up and examine?"

Touch the Sky felt the weight of their stares. His gaze met the mocking eyes of Wolf Who Hunts Smiling, the inscrutable gaze of Medicine Flute. One by one, he looked at the other warriors.

Only Tangle Hair and Little Horse did not avert their gazes. True, they were confused and did not understand how their friend Touch the Sky could know these things. But they had decided to stand with him no matter what.

Touch the Sky longed to reveal what Honey Eater had told him: the details explaining Medicine Flute's miracle, a miracle which in fact came straight from the white man's sky charts.

Then his eyes met the fierce, hateful stare of Black Elk. And those burning eyes reminded him that he could not say too much and let Black Elk suspect that Honey Eater warned him after overhearing the plan. For truly, Black Elk was already on the verge of killing her.

"Father," he finally answered, seeing which way the wind must set for the moment, "I cannot give you proof now. Perhaps later, but not now. So I promise this thing. No more will I publicly accuse Wolf Who Hunts Smiling of this crime."

"Good," Gray Thunder said, nodding. He cast a stern glance at Wolf Who Hunts Smiling. "And you, buck. You, too, are very free with your accusing mouth. I ask both of you to remember that only through the tribe do we live on. And a tribe divided cannot defend itself."

Wolf Who Hunts Smiling wiped the grin from his face. But his eyes still mocked Touch the Sky as he replied.

"Of course, Father. We are up against a powerful and clever foe. I shall do my part to keep my thoughts bloody against only them. I care only for the welfare of my people."

Big Tree and his Comanche warriors continued to drive their stolen ponies south. But the relentless pace had slowed. Grass was more sparse now, water holes fewer and farther between. Some of the water was alkali tainted, and great care had to be taken to keep the herd from drinking it.

Stone Club, keeping a constant eye on the swift-moving Cheyennes, reported that the war party must soon catch up with them. This news did not cause Big Tree undue concern. True, he was not eager for a fight, not against fanatical Northern Cheyennes. These north-country men knew only one style of battle—fighting until either they or their enemies were all dead.

The Comanches, in contrast, fought for the spoils of war. They did indeed glorify warfare, but dying in battle was not glorious. It was just death. They were indifferent to taking scalps or counting coups. Although revenge was sweet to them, as to most Indians, they placed little value on honor. An enemy killed in his sleep was just as dead as one killed on the battlefield.

Therefore, Big Tree planned to continue cooperating with Wolf Who Hunts Smiling. Of course, he would do so only insofar as such cooperation benefited him. But he differed from the wily Cheyenne on one important score. Wolf Who Hunts Smiling had apparently despaired of ever killing the tall shaman. Now he was content merely to destroy his standing as a medicine man, and thus his power as a leader.

Big Tree, in contrast, meant to kill Touch the Sky.

Well did he recall that night in a little canyon outside the shanty-and-sod hovel known as Over the River. The Comanches and their Kiowa allies were all set to trade their Cheyenne prisoners for a group of kidnapped white businessmen. But the businessmen turned out to be well-armed, disguised soldiers friendly to the Cheyennes. In the ensuing bloodbath, Big Tree had seen the Kiowa and Comanche leaders slain. And he himself had been knocked from his pony by the arrogant young Cheyenne shaman.

About midday, one sleep after the slaughter of the Cheyenne ponies, Rain in His Face rode up beside his leader.

"The ponies are tired. Gall has scouted forward and reports good grass near the Rio Mora. It would be smart to graze the herd there. Else we will arrive at the Blanco with skeletons."

Big Tree nodded. "Graze them. Then camp for the night. But move out even before the sun and make the best time you can. You are in charge until I return."

"Return? But, Quohada, where are you going?"

A grin split Big Tree's dust-coated face. Like his brothers, he wore his hair parted in the middle and just long enough to brush behind his ears. He was still a young man, but the sere Southwest sun had lined his face like the clay bed of a dried-up river.

"I am going to backtrack, brother. I am going to infiltrate the Cheyenne trail camp. And I am going to kill this tall Cheyenne who has left us the names of many dead who may no longer be mentioned."

It was a bold enough plan. But Rain in His Face showed little surprise. After all, next to their superb horsemanship, Comanches were best known for stealth. Like the Apaches, they were masters of concealment and subtle movement. It was said that not even shadows moved as smoothly as Comanches.

"Then kill him, Quohada."

Big Tree nodded. "I said I would. And when Big Tree speaks a thing, it is already done."

Trouble was in the wind. Some new threat was very close at hand. Touch the Sky sensed it.

Forward scouts reported they must soon overtake their enemy. That night, in their camp, the warriors attended to their battle rigs. As he tested the sinew string of his new bow, Touch the Sky constantly kept glancing out past the flickering tips of the fire.

"What is it, brother?" Little Horse said.

Touch the Sky stared into the blue-black maw of the night. The fine hairs on the back of his neck stood up.

"Nothing, buck," he finally replied. "Only a thing of smoke."

"It is this infernal flute playing," Tangle Hair said, staring past the fire toward the spot where Wolf Who Hunts Smiling sat with Medicine Flute. The flat, eerie notes of Medicine Flute's playing hovered over their camp like annoying birds.

"Straight words," Little Horse said. "This music would disturb the sleep of a dead man."

Touch the Sky nodded. But again a little tickle of premonition moved up his spine like an icy fingertip. He stared into the orbit vastness surrounding them, unable to shake the sense that tragedy loomed nearby.

Big Tree halted and dismounted well back from his enemy's camp. He hobbled his pony foreleg to rear with a short piece of rawhide. Then he prepared for the final and most dangerous leg of his journey.

He stripped completely naked and wallowed in a nearby muddy swale until his body was coated dark. Using short leather whangs, he tied broken-off bushes to his upper arms, legs, and back. Then, leaving most of his weapons with his mount, he selected only his osage-wood bow and one special Comanche arrow especially designed for victims sleeping on the ground.

The bow was so powerful it could drive a normal arrow through a buffalo's left flank, the arrow exiting cleanly from the right before falling on the ground. But this arrow Big Tree carried now was intended for cruelly pinning victims to the ground. The arrow point was cut from white man's pressed tin—a jagged, barbed point designed to tear and rip on its way through the victim, before biting deep into the ground under him.

He slipped the bow over his right shoulder, gripped the arrow in his mouth. Then he waited until the wind picked up, rustling the leaves in a ghostly whisper. Under cover of the noise he began creeping toward the Cheyenne camp, silent and smooth as the night shadows surrounding him.

Sentries had been posted and Medicine Flute had finally given over with his maddening music. The Cheyennes had drunk much water to ensure that aching bladders would wake them early. Now the fire had burned down to embers that glowed like eyes in the night.

As usual Touch the Sky had unrolled his buffalo robe near those of Little Horse and Tangle Hair. Soon he heard the steady, rhythmic breathing as they settled into sleep. But still, rest eluded him.

Beyond the silent camp circle, a coyote howled. An owl hooted, and far off in the distant foothills of the Red Hawk Mountains, Touch the Sky heard the ferocious kill cry of a mountain lion.

90

Nearby, a twig snapped, and Touch the Sky started up, his knife in his hand. But he relaxed when he saw it was just a fox sniffing at the scraps of meat from earlier.

But the snapping twig reminded him of a trick he had used to good effect in the past. Quietly, not disturbing the others, he gathered dried sticks and dead, crisp leaves, forming a little ring around his sleeping robe.

Still uneasy, but exhausted from the grueling pace of their mission, he finally settled into a fitful, uneasy sleep.

As the half-moon began to creep down from its zenith, Big Tree strung his special skewering arrow for the kill.

Slipping through the Cheyenne camp had been a risky business, and his heart was still pounding in his throat. But now his enemy lay on the ground before him, barely more than an arm's length away.

Big Tree pulled his bowstring taut, felt the long, sturdy bow give under the pressure. He aimed the longer-than-usual arrow and moved slightly for a better angle.

A stick crunched.

A heartbeat later, simultaneously, Big Tree launched his arrow and the barely alerted sleeper rolled hard to the right. But just before he bolted, the Comanche had the satisfaction of seeing his barbed-point arrow punch hard into his enemy's chest.

Chapter Eight

Little Horse thought, at first, that he must be dreaming.

Through thick cobwebs of deep sleep, he heard a gasping rattle that sounded like teeth being shaken hard in a gourd. It was the Sun Dance ceremony, he thought. Arrow Keeper must be keeping time for the high-kicking dancers.

But who was calling his name in that weak voice—a weak voice made tight and urgent with severe pain?

His eyes blinked open. Overhead, the star-shot heavens were vast and undisturbed. The camp was quiet except for the rhythmic cadence of the snoring Indians, the snuffling of their ponies tethered nearby under guard.

He heard again, faintly, the words charged

with horrendous pain. Someone calling his name.

He pulled his buffalo robe aside and sat up. Tangle Hair lay to his left, Touch the Sky on his right. He reached over to shake Touch the Sky awake, and his fingers brushed something warm and wet and sticky.

Then a breeze stirred, and he recognized the familiar odor of blood.

At that same moment a raft of clouds floated away from the moon, and Little Horse spotted the arrow that pinned his best friend to the ground like a stake.

Instinctively, his heart leaping into his throat, Little Horse raised the wolf howl, which to Cheyennes anywhere meant that their enemies were right on them. The next moment, dread heavy in every limb, he leaned over his friend to see if he was still among the living.

The fierce Black Elk was the first warrior to his feet, followed immediately by Tangle Hair.

"Who raised the alarm?" Black Elk demanded. He kicked up the embers.

"I did," Little Horse replied grimly. He had bent low over his friend and felt faint, warm breath on his eyelids. "Touch the Sky still lives, but he has been pinned by a Comanche long arrow!"

By now all the braves were awake, weapons to hand. All knew well what it meant to be pinned by the dreaded Comanche long arrow— almost certain death if the jagged-metal tip had gone through or even near vitals.

Touch the Sky's last-second roll spared him

from instant death, the pressed-tin point missing his heart by a hair. But his situation, trapped flat on the ground, was nearly hopeless. The buried point could not be snapped off behind him. This meant the arrow would have to be broken just above his chest. Then he would have to be lifted off the arrow. With the shaft—also notched to cut and tear—so close to the heart, this was as good as a death sentence.

"Never mind that," Black Elk said when a brave headed out beyond the circle of the fire. "These Comanche dogs may avoid open battles, but they are no cowards. This was the work of a lone brave. He has done it as a message of contempt. No attack is coming."

Wolf Who Hunts Smiling gaped in open astonishment. Could this thing be possible? Could the one man he hated more than any other possibly be treading the Death Path even now? This Big Tree—he had acted on his own, clearly, for this was not in the plan. Yet, it was a bold, rash, reckless act of courage. Thus it earned the wily Cheyenne's admiration.

He exchanged a secret glance with Medicine Flute. This brave, too, was fighting back a smirk of celebration. Both sensed that soon power would shift into their hands.

"New light is rimming the east," Gray Thunder said. "Black Elk, you are our battle leader. How do you counsel?"

"I am not one to stand about wringing my hands," Black Elk said. "Better to get them bloody! I say we ride out now."

He, too, was gloating as he listened to Touch the Sky's hard, uneven breathing. Black Elk recognized the early stages of the death rattle. This was the randy stallion who would mount his mare! Perhaps he had already topped Honey Eater. If so, surely he would never do so again.

"Ride out?" Little Horse stood and looked at the others. "Has a rabbit been wounded? Or is it the best warrior in the Cheyenne Nation?"

"I have ears for this," Tangle Hair said. "I would need to live two lifetimes to believe that Cheyenne warriors will coldly turn their backs on their own. Especially one who has bled for his tribe like this one has."

"Turn our backs?" Black Elk repeated scornfully. "Tangle Hair, I have never seen you hide in your tipi. With ten braves like you and Little Horse I could destroy ten times as many bluecoats.

"But, bucks, only use the eyes Maiyun gave you! Look there, how the pink bubbles flow from Touch the Sky's lips. He is hurt in his lights. And look at that long shaft. This one has been skewered by a Comanche long arrow. The metal point has torn his guts like bluecoat canister shot. If there is breath left in his nostrils, he had best sing the death song with it."

"This one," Wolf Who Hunts Smiling said, "is smoke behind us. The world belongs to the living, Cheyennes! Let us ride. Little Horse, all you have left for your grief is revenge. Ride with us, stout brave, and we will dangle Comanche scalps from our coup sticks."

"The world belongs to the living," Little Horse repeated with contempt. "You speak from two mouths, Panther Clan. Touch the Sky once told me a thing. He told me how your cousin Black Elk sent you and Swift Canoe to murder Touch the Sky while he was on his vision quest at Medicine Lake.

"And indeed you tried. Even so, Touch the Sky saved you when, on your way back to camp, Pawnees attacked you. And now you would leave him like so much dressed-out meat!"

Chief Gray Thunder knew nothing of this story. Now he stared at Black Elk and Wolf Who Hunts Smiling, waiting for a denial.

But they both wisely held their silence. For the murderous anger in Little Horse's eyes would brook no more slighting of his friend. If any warrior could fight as an equal beside Touch the Sky, it was surely Little Horse. No one present was eager to cross lances with him when he had blood in his eyes as he did now.

"While we talk," Black Elk said, "our enemies drive our ponies closer to the impregnable Blanco Canyon. This is a war party. Therefore we are not guided by rules of council, but by my commands. And I say we ride."

"Do as you will." Little Horse had knelt beside his friend again. "I stay with this fallen warrior, the man I consider our tribe's best."

"We could use you, buck," Black Elk said. "But despite your insolence, I will not hold you in violation of my orders. I admire you too much."

And for a moment, just a few heartbeats, Little Horse saw Black Elk's face soften a bit as he looked at the supine Touch the Sky.

"And as you say, this is a warrior. I trained him. I confess, he was so mired in white man's ignorance that I was sure the training would kill him within five sleeps. But Cheyenne blood will eventually out, and he has since covered this tribe in glory more than once. Now he must soon cross over to the Land of Ghosts. But I promise that he will be carried to his scaffold wearing new moccasins and with all his weapons about him."

"One world at a time," Little Horse said grimly, turning his back on the rest as they prepared to ride. "He has not left this one yet."

The war party rode out, faces blackened with charcoal. And once again Touch the Sky's fate was in his best friend's hands.

Little Horse knew that his companion's life was balanced on the edge of a feather. Just as his own had been when the bluecoat Seth Carlson shot him near the Milk River. And hadn't Touch the Sky pulled him back from the very jaws of death into the world of the living?

Little Horse dreaded what had to be done immediately. Lifting Touch the Sky off that arrow would be one of the hardest acts Little Horse had ever performed. And not just because his friend was big. That long shaft had been deliberately barbed and notched to rip and tear. The damage already done might have been fatal.

How could the unconscious warrior possibly survive another pass through his body?

Although morning light streaked the eastern sky, Little Horse built up the fire. He said a simple battle prayer to focus his courage. Then, working with great care, he used his knife to cut through the shaft of the arrow where it protruded from Touch the Sky's chest.

His friend still breathed, but barely—the rapid, shallow panting of a dying animal. Little Horse knelt, opened his parfleche, and removed several twists of fine white man's tobacco. He scattered it to the directions of the wind as a gift to Maiyun, the Great Medicine Man.

Little Horse owned a beautiful Indian saddle, recently obtained in a trade with one of Chief Bull Hump's Dakotas. It was flat, beautifully embroidered with Sioux beadwork, his favorite possession and the envy of his clan. Not once hesitating, he now uncinched it from his horse and completely shredded it with his knife. Thus, he hoped, his sacrifice would give wings to his prayer for Touch the Sky.

Finally, it was time. He knelt, slid both arms carefully under his friend, and planted his feet firmly. He inhaled a huge breath, expelled it, then took another. His heart pulsed hard in his ears.

"Today, brother," he said out loud to his companion, "is not a good day to die!

"Hi-ya, hiii-ya!"

Screaming the fierce war cry of his tribe, Little Horse strained to rise. His well-muscled thighs and calves went taut, but at first the arrow refused to let go of its victim.

Summoning strength he never realized he had, the short but stocky warrior gasped with supreme effort. Veins in his neck swelled up like fat blue nightcrawlers, his arms trembled, and he felt a slow giving away of tension. Then, just as he was sure he must collapse, he felt his friend slide up and off the arrow.

But Little Horse felt little elation even as he gently laid his brother in his open buffalo robe. True, his friend's harsh grunt of pain proved he was still alive. But he had glimpsed that shaft—what remained of it—in the new light. And it was covered with bloody gobbets of gut and flesh.

For two full sleeps Little Horse tended to his friend, doing his best to confound death.

He heated his knife blade in the embers and cauterized the entrance and exit wounds. He made a paste of river mud, gunpowder, and balsam, binding the wounds with strips of cypress bark. Touch the Sky alternated between burning fevers and bone-numbing chills.

At first he could take no nourishment except sips of water. Everything else he vomited up. Little Horse stole wild peas from the caches of field mice. These he cooked and then mashed with his knife, mixing it with bone marrow. Touch the Sky was able to hold this concoction down.

Though he passed in and out of consciousness, his talk was wild and dreamlike, that of a man gone Wendigo. Then, on the third day after the long arrow pierced him, Touch the Sky's eyes opened wide.

"Brother," he said weakly to his friend, "cook some meat. I would eat like a living man!"

Later that night, over Little Horse's objections, Touch the Sky decided they would ride out next morning. The sun was still rising, Touch the Sky moving slowly and carefully, when they cut sign on the others and set out.

Chapter Nine

"Cousin," Black Elk said, "I regret that a Comanche arrow did what we could not. Still, Woman Face has been sent under. I could not wish the deed undone."

"I have ears for this, Cheyenne. Long have I dreamed of burying my tomahawk in his skull. But he has been sent under. This is one kill I do not begrudge our enemies."

Black Elk, leading his war party, had dropped back to ride beside his cousin. The land was more barren—buttes and mesas and redrock canyons with grass sparse away from the rivers. The pace had been considerably slowed for the fleeing Comanches and their stolen pony herd. Now the Cheyennes could spot their dust trail far out above the horizon.

"A thing troubles me," Black Elk said.

Wolf Who Hunts Smiling had prepared for this. He had noticed his cousin brooding more and more, and he knew what was coming.

"Then speak this thing," he said.

"It concerns Medicine Flute. I was present when plans were made to play the fox with this miracle of the burning star. It was a good plan and worked well. Only, tell me a thing. Tell me about this business with the pony ribs sticking from the ground. How could he have had this vision without cooperating with our enemies? Surely he is not truly blessed with big medicine. A true shaman would never have lied about the burning star."

Black Elk's face was stern. Though he had gone so far to make Touch the Sky's life miserable—even sullying the Sacred Arrows by trying to kill him—he could never be a traitor to his tribe. Nor would he tolerate such behavior in any Cheyenne.

Wolf Who Hunts Smiling knew this. Now he said, "Cousin, I could tell you it was Medicine Flute's magic. But I will not. Only think. Do you know where Swift Canoe is?"

Black Elk's face was blank. "No. Nor do I care. Why should I? He is back at camp, I would wager. But—" He cut himself off as his cousin's meaning dawned on him. "You had him secretly scout ahead?"

Wolf Who Hunts Smiling grinned. "I did. I confess I played the fox on my own. Medicine Flute had a good description, indeed."

This evoked a rare smile from the stern war

leader. "So that is the way the wind sets. Good work, buck!"

Relief surging through him, Wolf Who Hunts Smiling congratulated himself for this successful deception. Black Elk, never one for schemes, had been readily fooled. This was important. For truly Wolf Who Hunts Smiling found himself walking a fine line. Granted, Touch the Sky was no doubt dead or dying. This was a source of great personal pleasure as well as essential to his plans for someday leading his own red nation in a war of extermination against the palefaces. Touch the Sky had been the greatest obstacle to those plans.

But Touch the Sky aside, Wolf Who Hunts Smiling still needed Big Tree as an ally. The young Cheyenne's ambition was as wide as the plains themselves. He wisely understood, however, the one great weakness of the red man: any real lack of unity. Tribe warred upon tribe, weakening their potential to combine and deal the bluecoats a massive death blow.

Big Tree was the key to gaining an important southern plains ally. But that meant Wolf Who Hunts Smiling must purchase the fierce Comanche's loyalty. To his own tribe, Wolf Who Hunts Smiling must appear eager to defeat these Comanche raiders; but, in fact, he knew he must subvert his tribe so their enemy might escape. That was his agreement with Big Tree.

Black Elk chucked up his pony, resuming his spot at the head of his war party. But several times Wolf Who Hunts Smiling saw his cousin turn to stare back toward him.

Then he realized that Black Elk was looking well beyond him—staring farther behind, as if he still could not believe that Woman Face was worm fodder.

"Brother, this hard pace is making fresh blood flow from your wounds," Little Horse said. "Let us make a camp for the night."

The two friends had stopped to water their ponies in a small runoff stream. Their sister, the sun, had gone to her resting place, leaving the vast night sky to Uncle Moon.

Touch the Sky shook his head. "It is only a spot of blood. The moon is full, the stars many. Light is good, so let us keep riding."

"Buck," Little Horse said, impatience creeping into his tone, "I admire your stout heart, surely. But what good is it to kill yourself playing the hero?"

"I play at nothing. We must hurry. Wolf Who Hunts Smiling and Medicine Flute have become dogs for these Comanches. If we let the grass grow under us now, our pony herd is lost. Perhaps our comrades are, too."

Little Horse narrowed his eyes, watching his tall friend closely in the generous moonwash. Yes, his face was drawn and pinched with pain, dust-streaked from the grueling pace. Touch the Sky was still weak from loss of blood. But there was also an odd, determined glint in his eyes—a look Little Horse had seen before. Better to bait a grizzly, he told himself, than defy that glint.

"Brother," he said quietly, "I have seen the

mark of the arrow buried past your hairline. Arrow Keeper has spoken to me about the meaning of this mark, about his vision that foretold you would be a great leader.

"I have also seen this light like fox fire in your eyes. The hand of the supernatural is in this thing. That Comanche arrow should have killed you, but Maiyun willed otherwise. So if you say we ride, then, Cheyenne, we ride!"

Medicine Flute's eerie music finally fell silent. Wolf Who Hunts Smiling feigned sleep until all of his comrades were snoring around him. Then, silent as the stalking wolf for which he was named, he slipped from his buffalo robes.

Earlier they had met up with River of Winds. According to the scout's report, they would overtake their enemy on the morrow. But Wolf Who Hunts Smiling had no intention of letting this happen.

The ponies were tethered in a grassy draw just north of camp, under guard as always. Wolf Who Hunts Smiling now took a lesson from the Comanche. He found a fist-size rock and wrapped it tight in rawhide.

The guard was Tangle Hair. But Wolf Who Hunts Smiling had no intention of killing him if he could avoid it. His faith in the Medicine Arrows was weak. However, the Cheyenne taboo against slaying fellow Cheyennes was strong and affected him, too. He did not consider Touch the Sky a true Cheyenne, so the taboo did not apply to him. But letting Comanches kill the herd guards, on that night of the miracle, was as far as he cared to go.

Now he told himself that a good tap to the skull would suffice to silence Tangle Hair for a bit. He would then drop the rawhide-wrapped rock beside him as proof Comanches did it.

The land here was sandy. So Wolf Who Hunts Smiling was careful to walk on his heels. He wanted no telltale prints leading back to his sleeping robes.

He waited for gusts of wind to cover the sound of his movements. Tangle Hair was no brave to be taken lightly, one of the best of the Bow String troopers. But the brave would not be looking for trouble from the direction of camp.

Finally Wolf Who Hunts Smiling spotted him. Tangle Hair was seated at the crest of a small hill, his vigilant eyes directed toward the south. Wolf Who Hunts Smiling stopped breathing through his nose—this was too much noise around a brave as sharp as Tangle Hair.

He crept closer, raised the rock, and swung it into Tangle Hair's left temple. There was a sickening thud. A heartbeat later, Tangle Hair lay sprawled on the ground.

Grinning with elation, Wolf Who Hunts Smiling glided smooth as a shadow into the midst of the ponies. Familiar with his smell, they only snorted in friendly greeting.

He stooped and quickly began removing their tethers.

It was Little Horse's keen sense of smell that first told them they were about to overtake the camp of their companions.

He had stopped his mount to carefully sniff the wind.

"Ponies ahead," he said. They had already cut sign on their comrades and knew from the number of riders that it must be the Cheyennes.

"Brother," Touch the Sky said, "I have no desire to rouse the entire camp when they are painted for battle. There will be a pony guard out. Let us slip up on the camp and give him the owl hoot so he will not wake the rest and get us killed for Comanches."

Little Horse nodded. He sniffed the wind again. Then he led them up a long bluff. Below, in the silver-white moonlight, they saw the grazing ponies. However, they could not yet spot the guard.

Touch the Sky imitated an owl hoot, the Cheyenne way of signaling the approach of a friend. At first, nothing. But after he did it again, the signal was returned.

"Good. He knows we are here," Touch the Sky said.

"Give me your hackamore, brother," Little Horse said. "You are so tired even your voice is weary. Go roll into your buffalo robe while I tether our mounts. Get what little sleep remains for this night."

Touch the Sky was indeed too exhausted to argue with this. His wounded chest throbbed mightily. He was halfway down the draw, threading his way through the ponies, when he noticed that several of the ponies were drifting away from the group, farther than

Judd Cole

normal tethers would allow. Before the meaning of this could sink in, he almost tripped over something.

He glanced down and recognized Tangle Hair in the moonlight.

Blood matted the left side of his forehead, but fortunately his breathing was still strong. Wincing at the pain in his own chest, Touch the Sky knelt to take a closer look. Satisfied his friend would live, the Cheyenne rose again and prepared to raise the wolf howl of alarm. But who, he thought, had answered his signal?

That was when he spotted a lone figure off to his right. The intruder had knelt and was staring back toward the camp.

No doubt another Comanche. Clearly this was a lone raider. Now Touch the Sky understood why there had been such a long pause before his owl hoot was answered. This wily enemy had given the response, not a Cheyenne.

Touch the Sky knew the interloper might well escape if he raised the wolf howl. His mind calculated quickly. He was armed only with his obsidian knife, having left his other weapons in his pony rigging for Little Horse to carry. Touch the Sky knew he was too weak for a sustained battle. But if he could capitalize on the element of surprise. . . .

He slid his knife from its beaded sheath and moved in closer. He was perhaps a double arm's length from striking range when his foot suddenly startled a fat gopher snake. It streaked off, rustling the grass, and the crouching figure suddenly rose and whirled around.

"You!" Wolf Who Hunts Smiling gaped in wide-eyed astonishment. It was he who had answered the owl hoot, unsure who had made it. But in the clear moonlight, there was no mistaking his enemy's broad shoulders and the grim, determined slit of his mouth.

Touch the Sky, fully expecting a Comanche warrior, was equally surprised.

"Once again, White Man Runs Him, you have outfoxed death. Notice, this time I do not tremble as I did when you outwitted the grizzly. I see from that blood on your chest that you are a man of flesh and bone."

This was a reference to the time when Wolf Who Hunts Smiling and Swift Canoe had lured a ravenous grizzly to Touch the Sky's cave at Medicine Lake. Convinced his foe must be dead and returned as a spirit, Wolf Who Hunts Smiling had begged for his life when his enemy appeared before him.

"You still had some decency left in you then," Touch the Sky replied. "You could have killed me. But you didn't because you still respected the Sacred Arrows. That decency you once had is gone, as this further act of treachery against your own tribe proves. You know these ponies are still wild and will run when the tether is slipped."

"I know many things, Woman Face! I know that I only spared your life because there was still a soft place in my heart. But it is all rock now, buck."

"No, you are wrong there. For a rock cannot be a traitor to its own, Comanche dog!"

In a moment Wolf Who Hunts Smiling's knife was in his hand. Clearly, his enemy was exhausted, weakened, in no condition to fight. And had Woman Face not already boldly announced, at council, no less, that he intended to kill him?

Reading Wolf Who Hunts Smiling's eyes close, Touch the Sky also gleaned his enemy's thoughts.

"Yes," he said, "I announced I was going to kill you. For after all, it was you who first walked between me and the campfire, saying to all that you would send me under. And now you play the dog for those who stole our women and children, killed our elders. The Cheyenne way does not permit murder of our own. But it also decrees that a traitor ceases to be a Cheyenne. Your blood cannot stain the Arrows."

"I have no ears for you. You have knocked Death from his pony more times than I can count. And I chafed, thinking Big Tree had deprived me of the pleasure of killing you. But now, like the ponies I just set free, your luck has reached the end of its tether!"

A heartbeat later, his blade glinting cruelly in a shaft of moonlight, Wolf Who Hunts Smiling leaped on his enemy.

Chapter Ten

Wolf Who Hunts Smiling was small. But he was hard knit, quick, and surprisingly strong, and once he bridged the gap, his every instinct led straight for the kill.

Knowing he was too weak to overpower Wolf Who Hunts Smiling in his present condition, Touch the Sky did not try to resist. Instead, he fell in the direction of the attack. Pain jolted through his wounded chest as he hit the ground. But the unexpected lack of resistance sent Wolf Who Hunts Smiling tumbling head over heels behind him.

Touch the Sky scrambled to his feet, slower than usual. Just in the nick of time he managed to spin around and meet the second assault.

He twisted sideways, feeling his enemy's blade slice his ribs as it ripped through his leather shirt. Already Touch the Sky was breathing hard from his exertions. Desperate, he swept his left leg in a wide arc and hooked it behind one of Wolf Who Hunts Smiling's legs. A moment later, the smaller brave crashed to the ground on his back, literally swept off his feet. He grunted in surprise.

By now several of the ponies, agitated by the commotion, were nickering in nervous fright. Touch the Sky's chest wound bled freely. He raised his knife and fell on top of his enemy, seeking warm vitals and a final end to this long rivalry. But the powerful brave instantly arched his back hard, rolling Touch the Sky clear.

With a snarl of wild triumph, Wolf Who Hunts Smiling leaped atop his weakened adversary. Touch the Sky barely managed to grab his opponent's arm in time to stop it before the knife sank deep into his neck. Now the razor-sharp edge of the blade was poised only a few hairs away from his throat as Touch the Sky pitted his brawn against Wolf Who Hunts Smiling's.

At first it was a standoff, death held at bay but only an eye blink away. But then slowly, inexorably, the blade began to press into flesh as Touch the Sky's exhausted reserves of strength rapidly gave out.

"Die, Woman Face!" Wolf Who Hunts Smiling taunted him as a line of blood appeared on his victim's neck. "Perform your strong medicine now, shaman!"

Pain was a white-hot crease across his neck.

Touch the Sky felt the blade sinking deeper. A few more heartbeats and his trembling arms would collapse. Then his throat would be ripped open like a second mouth. But a moment later, Wolf Who Hunts Smiling was lifted off of him.

"Buck," Chief Gray Thunder said with angry authority, "you are on the feather edge of murdering your own! Had the ponies not woken me, you would have the putrid stink of the murderer on you for life. Do you sully the Arrows even as we pursue an enemy? Do you risk Maiyun's wrath at a time when we need His benevolence most?"

The powerful chief's face was hatchet sharp in his anger.

"But," Wolf Who Hunts Smiling said, "you do not understand! I caught Woman Fa—Touch the Sky scattering our horses! Do you not see? Clearly this is an act of revenge. He is angered because Medicine Flute's true magic has exposed his sham medicine. This act of treachery was meant to suggest that Medicine Flute cannot protect us."

By now, alerted by the noise, the rest of the braves had formed a circle around them.

"Touch the Sky," Gray Thunder said, "are these words straight? You were hurt deep in your lights and we gave you up for dead. Perhaps we did wrong in leaving, but we had an enemy to pursue. Is this how you exact revenge?"

"Father, I have exacted nothing. Once again this wolf lives up to his name. He was scattering the ponies! I say it again. Wolf Who Hunts Smiling is drinking from the same pond as Big Tree and his Comanches."

This set the warriors buzzing. Many found both stories hard to believe.

Little Horse edged his way through the circle and spoke up. "Touch the Sky speaks straight arrow. We had just arrived in camp. I was turning our ponies out to graze, and he was heading toward the camp to sleep."

"Did you see Wolf Who Hunts Smiling turning loose our ponies?" Chief Gray Thunder demanded of Little Horse.

Reluctantly, the sturdy little brave shook his head. Touch the Sky watched Wolf Who Hunts Smiling and Medicine Flute exchange a knowing glance.

"Tangle Hair has been hurt!" a brave named Battle Sash called over. "He is coming to now. I think he will be all right. He has been hit with a rock."

A few moments later, Battle Sash led a stumbling Tangle Hair over to join the others.

"Brother," Gray Thunder said, "did you see who hit you?"

Tangle Hair shook his head. "Whoever it was came from the direction of camp."

Tangle Hair had turned accusing eyes on Wolf Who Hunts Smiling. "I suspect this one! He is a Bull Whip, and they are not close friends with honor."

"I, too, am a Bull Whip," Black Elk said hotly. "Would you insult my honor?"

"Enough of this clash of bulls," Gray Thun-

der said. "What has this tribe come to? Our
enemy lies just ahead, with the best pony herd
we have captured in recent memory. And here
we stand, making war faces against one another. You"—he turned to Touch the Sky—"once
again you have accused Wolf Who Hunts Smiling of traitorous behavior. And once again you
cannot prove the charge. Do you offer even
one bit of evidence we may pick up and examine?"

Touch the Sky bit back his words and merely shook his head. The only course open to
him was to explain what Honey Eater had told
him—how she had overheard the plot hatched
that night behind Black Elk's meat racks. Honey Eater was greatly respected. If she swore
to these things on the Arrows or the Buffalo
Hat, she would be believed. But her life would
be forfeit, for Black Elk's jealous pride would
never brook such behavior from her.

"And, you," the chief said, whirling to stare
at Wolf Who Hunts Smiling. "You are no better. You say Touch the Sky was freeing our
ponies, and you, too, lack any proof. Now your
chief says this to both of you. There is no council present. This is not a matter for Black Elk,
as battle chief, to decide. So now your peace
chief speaks, and you had both best have ears
for my words.

"I have my eyes on both of you. For truly,
one of you is a traitor. And I swear by the
sun and the earth I live on, when I discover which of the two it is, he will die a dog's
death!"

*   *   *

"Quohada, are you telling me my long arrow did not kill the tall young buck?" Big Tree said.

Stone Club nodded. The secret messenger had just returned from a hasty conference with Wolf Who Hunts Smiling.

"He is weak but alive. The Cheyennes are divided now. Some follow the thin shaman with the bone flute; others are loyal to the tall one. According to the Wolf Who Hunts Smiling, their chief knows not what to believe. And even now they are riding hard to meet us."

Big Tree was so incensed that his nostrils flared. He sat his stocking-footed chestnut on a long, rocky spine south of the Smoky Hill River. They had paused briefly to graze the ponies for the long haul across the barren panhandle country of Texas. Now his band was pointing the herd to resume the trek.

How, Big Tree wondered yet again, had the Cheyenne survived? It had been a good hit with a deadly arrow. Could the stories be true? Was his life charmed, protected by magic? But, no, it must have been when he rolled at the last moment. Somehow that fateful roll kept the arrow from striking to the quick of him.

"Wolf Who Hunts Smiling has sent a message," Stone Club added. "He has a new plan. When we reach the Red River, we are to select six more of the ponies, slaughter them, and leave them by the trail. He said to be sure that their eyes are gouged out. He promises that this time his tribe will turn against the tall one."

Slowly, Big Tree nodded. The silver conchos on his tall shako hat reflected in the bright sunlight, as did the bits of broken mirror embedded in his rawhide shield. Gradually a grin replaced his frown as he realized his wily Cheyenne ally was up to yet more treachery.

"Good," he said. "We will do it. I have no desire to waste good horses. And yet, if it hurts us, how must it make those pony-loving fools feel?"

Big Tree had no respect for a tribe that permitted its men only one wife each. And unlike the Comanches, Cheyenne braves were not permitted to slaughter their wives for cause—even if the woman was caught lying with another man! No wonder they practically worshiped their horses; they were sentimental fools. Cowards, no, but sentimental fools. And Big Tree had learned long ago that the more things a man loved the more ways he could be hurt.

"Now we ride hard," Big Tree said. "They will catch up to us soon enough. But when they reach the Red River and see what we have left for them, they will certainly pause."

Despite the loyalty of Little Horse, Tangle Hair, and a few others, Touch the Sky could feel the hostility of many in the war party.

Their slanted glances and quiet remarks showed that many had accepted Wolf Who Hunts Smiling's story that Touch the Sky had attempted to scatter their ponies. Many had made a great show of expressing friendship toward Medicine Flute, a brave hitherto

117

mostly ignored. Only the hard pace across the barren plains kept them too distracted to act on their suspicions—that and Chief Gray Thunder's clear desire to remain neutral and let the truth uncover itself.

"Brother," Little Horse said, riding beside his friend, "keep your senses stronger than your thoughts and your weapons to hand. Tangle Hair and I have already discussed this thing, and we are sworn to death beside you if it comes to that. We both agree that it is better to die like men, free warriors, than to play the dog for the likes of Wolf Who Hunts Smiling and Medicine Flute.

"Certain others agree with us. But they will not speak out now and encourage dissension. Not now, as we are closing for battle against a tribal enemy. But the fight is finally at hand, brother. I feel it."

Touch the Sky nodded. He rode the tough little bay, his new white mare with her silky gray mane following on a lead line. "It is closing fast upon us. Wolf Who Hunts Smiling and his Bull Whip brothers have set things in motion, things that cannot be undone. The tribe as we know it will soon be no more. And those who survive the bloody battles to come will be forced to choose not just a leader, but life or death."

Even as he spoke, Touch the Sky spotted Black Elk and Wolf Who Hunts Smiling staring at him.

"But for now, brother," he added, "I follow your advice. The future of our tribe is not the matter. I listen to the language of my senses,

not to thoughts. And you must do the same,
for they now understand that an attack against
either of us is a fight with both of us."

Forward scouts confirmed that the fight
would be soon, probably soon after the next rising of the sun. The Cheyenne warriors planned
to rest their ponies well when they reached
the Red River, then mount a classic running
battle—the type of warfare they excelled in.

Though they knew Comanche scouts had an
eye on them, they made a cold camp on the
night before they reached the Red River. Black
Elk chose a site just east of the rolling region
whites called Purgatory Hills, a grassy flat in
the lee of a mesa.

The guard was doubled, the rest of the braves
tending to their battle rigs. By now hardly anyone bothered to notice when Medicine Flute's
eerie music began.

But all did notice when it abruptly halted in
midnote.

And all stared, jaws dropping in astonishment, when the young shaman's eyes went wide
in terror. He no longer blinked, but seemed not
to focus his gaze on any scene in this world. He
sat cross-legged and rigid in the last of the
sun's weak rays; the leg-bone flute had rolled
from his fingers and dropped unnoticed to the
ground.

He did not have to request their attention, as
braves normally did. When his words rang out,
they had the force of supernatural authority
commanding them.

"Had I the choice, I would never have been born to see what I must see now for the sake of my people!"

"Hold fast, brothers," Touch the Sky whispered to Little Horse and Tangle Hair. "More wolf barks."

"Our tribe has blindly followed a false shaman!" Medicine Flute called out. "Now Maiyun is sending us a sign that we must pay for that blindness. What I have just seen, I have no heart to describe. Only wait until we reach the Red River, brothers, and you will see what our blindness has done!"

Chapter Eleven

The Cheyenne warriors rode out from their cold camp well before the sun had risen. Black Elk sent out point and flank riders, each equipped with a fragment of mirror for communicating with the main war party.

The rolling plains had given way to flat, unvarying country with only the occasional redrock butte or sandstone formation to break the monotony. Ahead, they could see the lingering, yellow-brown columns of dust raised by their stolen herd.

There was great excitement—tinged with dread—about Medicine Flute's cryptic and dramatic prediction. But by now Touch the Sky knew full well the prediction would indeed come true. He had no doubt that Big Tree and

Wolf Who Hunts Smiling had secretly teamed up to ensure this.

River of Winds had been sent forward on point. Soon after sunrise he returned, his face a grim mask. He spoke privately with Gray Thunder and Black Elk. But he only shook his head in mute refusal when the rest asked him what he had seen. He made a point, however, of avoiding eye contact with Touch the Sky.

"Notice, bucks," Little Horse said to Touch the Sky and Tangle Hair, "that Wolf Who Hunts Smiling has not troubled to speak with River of Winds as the rest are doing. He is not even curious to know what he saw."

"Why should he be?" Touch the Sky said. "River of Winds can only tell him what he already knows. Arrow Keeper was right. The red man's faith in visions can too often be cruelly exploited. Soon, I fear, we will be up against more trouble.

"Therefore, look sharp, Cheyennes! You have chosen to cast your lot with mine, and now my enemies are yours, too. We three must ride close and cover each other; we must watch for the attack. This vision has been devised in hopes of finally turning the rest against us. We must make it clear we will sell our souls dearly."

Finally, with the morning still young, the war party spotted the scattered cottonwoods of a river valley ahead. They crested the last long rise and saw sunlight glinting off the quick-flowing water of the Red River.

"There!" Black Elk called out grimly. He

pointed to the left of the trail they were following.

The gleaming, mutilated pony corpses had already drawn a swarm of flies, and the first carrion birds had quit circling and were beginning to land.

"Look!" Wolf Who Hunts Smiling called out when he had ridden closer. "Only look, brothers! Their eyes have been cut out. Did Medicine Flute not say that our blindness in following a false shaman has caused all this trouble? Now, look how the eyeless ponies themselves give powerful testimony to this same fact!"

"Brothers!" Black Elk called out. "How much proof do we need of Medicine Flute's powerful magic? Touch the Sky has not described one vision to us!"

"Because he is a pretend shaman!" the Bull Whip named Snake Eater called out. "Just as he is a pretend Cheyenne."

This time, with the eyeless ponies lying in mute accusation, more braves spoke out against Touch the Sky.

"Our mistake was in listening to Arrow Keeper. That one dotes on this tall one. He said this Touch the Sky would train for a medicine man. Once he spoke, all critics were silenced!"

"How much harm has it cost us? How many times has this pretend shaman led the Renewal of the Arrows, and we believed there was medicine in it?"

"How angry have we made the High Holy Ones?" Wolf Who Hunts Smiling shouted. "Is it a thing to wonder at, that we have lost our fine ponies? And how can we expect to get them back when we ride into battle with no medicine? Indeed, with the bad medicine of white men and their dogs?"

This was a serious thought, indeed, and every warrior was silent. A typical Cheyenne brave would face any danger—even certain death— if he were properly dressed and painted, if his shield and lance were blessed with strong medicine. But stout warriors were not considered cowards when they ran away from battle because they had no medicine. For dying without medicine meant eternal darkness and solitude in the Forest of Tears. And no Indian feared anything more than he feared solitude.

Chief Gray Thunder was about to speak up, but Wolf Who Hunts Smiling sensed blood in the wind, and he took a bold chance.

"Brothers, have ears! This is three times now that Medicine Flute has proven his strong medicine. Do you realize what we have done? We have been following a false shaman! We have let a white man's dog touch our Sacred Arrows! This White Man Runs Him, he has the stink on him that scares off the buffalo herds. Yet, we have let him chant the cure songs and lead the Animal Dance!"

Quietly, as they had arranged, Touch the Sky, Little Horse, and Tangle Hair maneuvered their ponies until the three braves formed a sort of triangle. With the river running before them, Touch the Sky faced the right flank, Little Horse the left, and Tangle Hair covered the rear. They knew what was coming, and it did.

"Cheyenne brothers!" Wolf Who Hunts Smiling shouted. "We have no choice but the honorable deed! This Touch the Sky, aided by his allies, has destroyed our tribe's medicine. We ride to certain death against the Comanches unless we appease the High Holy Ones. We must execute this pretend shaman, or else we are lost!"

He thrust his streamered lance high overhead, and many braves followed suit, raising the war cry. But even as they turned to face the trio, Touch the Sky spoke up.

"Hold, and have ears for my words now! This Wolf Who Hunts Smiling, what manner of leader is he? Does he wear the Buffalo Hat? Has he been elected a headman? Is he your war chief or the leader of a soldier society? No, he is none of these things. Yet, you all listen to him as if his words had authority behind them.

"His words are lies, as black as his heart. A Cheyenne can put nothing before the welfare of his tribe. Yet this ambitious young liar, lusting for power and a bloody, senseless war against the hair faces, has made a mockery of the Cheyenne way. He speaks of a false shaman. Yet you who follow him follow a false god, for truly he has set himself up as a god.

"And now I say this. Things are the way they are. Look close, all of you, and notice that three of the best warriors in your tribe are now prepared to sing the death song. We have defeated hair-faced soldiers, Pawnees, Crows, Comanches, and Kiowas. Our coup feathers, trailed together, would stretch from where I stand now to the Land Beyond the Sun! We challenge any brave to bridge the gap, for we are ready. Perhaps you will kill us. But tuck these words in your sashes. Many will cross over for each of us you kill, and the widows will wail for many moons after we three have done our bloody best."

These sobering words took the blood out of more than one warrior's eyes. Now Gray Thunder spoke before Wolf Who Hunts Smiling could retort.

"Now your chief is speaking! This decision to execute a Cheyenne has nothing to do with our present battle. Therefore, it is not a matter for Black Elk or his hotheaded young cousin to decree. Black Elk, as war leader, makes all battle decisions. But I, as your peace chief, decide other matters in the absence of the Council of Forty.

"Look at those three! Look at their faces! Are those white-liverd cowards or are they warriors to be reckoned with? Touch the Sky spoke well. A dear price will be exacted for their blood. Now stop all this foolish talk of killing our own. We came to rescue our ponies. Those who are thirsty for blood will find plenty to drink when we catch up with Big Tree. But so long as we stand here, fighting among ourselves, the Comanches have nothing to fear.

"Black Elk, be a man! Take charge of your warriors and let us raise our battle cry as one tribe!"

This speech met with a rousing cheer from almost every Cheyenne present except Wolf

Who Hunts Smiling and Medicine Flute. Black
Elk nodded once, approving his chief's wisdom.
Then he led his men in fording the river, and the
chase was on.

Big Tree was seething with rage.

Wolf Who Hunts Smiling—had he not assured Big Tree that the tall one would be worm
fodder by now? And yet the report from Stone
Club was as clear as a blood spoor in new snow.
The Cheyenne war party was closing upon them
fast, and the arrogant young shaman rode with
them.

"Truly," Stone Club added, "this tall warrior
is a difficult one to catch by the throat. Some
of our men, Quohada, are saying things. They
are saying this shaman truly is the Bear Caller
of Pawnee nightmares, his vitality beyond the
power of mortal weapons."

Stone Club stopped short, but Big Tree understood his hint clearly enough. A Comanche war
leader was respected most for ability in combat.
His braves had a right to expect him to demonstrate that superior ability in a contest with
the best warrior the Cheyennes could send out.
Comanches loved entertainment, be it a torture
session or a good duel to the death between
well-matched bucks.

Big Tree knew his power as an Indian leader
lay in his seeming invincibility. He must con-
front the Cheyenne dog in single combat.

"Stone Club, next time you hear the men
saying these things, tell them this. Tell them
the Bear Caller may indeed be beyond the pow-

er of mortal weapons. But ask them if mortal weapon has yet brought down their leader, Big Tree?

"Say this, Stone Club. Many Comanches were there when the Bear Caller killed our leader and then tried to kill Big Tree. He gave it his supernatural best, yet only knocked Big Tree from his horse. Big Tree falls from his horse when he is drunk! This is nothing.

"And finally, do certainly say this. Say that no red man on the plains can outride or outfight Big Tree. Say that a word-bringer has been sent back under a truce flag to meet with the Cheyennes. Say, too, that Big Tree challenges this tall Cheyenne shaman to mounted combat with battle lances and war clubs only. The winner keeps the pony herd."

It was the brave named Rain in His Face who took the message to the Cheyennes. He spoke enough Sioux words to make himself understood, using sign talk when all else failed.

Black Elk turned to Gray Thunder when the message was delivered. But their chief only shrugged. "This is a warrior's decision, not a peace leader's. However, we came to get our ponies. We must get them if possible, but not forget that we also came to avenge the blood of our dead herd guards."

Black Elk and the rest understood Gray Thunder's meaning. In agreeing to the contest, he was not also promising to ride the peace path. Big Tree had not demanded that. Their word of honor would mean, of course, that they would surrender the herd if Touch the Sky lost. But they would be free to attack at any time afterward, for blood vengeance was a separate issue.

Black Elk looked to his cousin and Medicine Flute. At first, this unexpected move left Wolf Who Hunts Smiling as surprised as the rest. This Big Tree, his new ally—he was turning out to be as unpredictable as the Blackfoot warrior Sis-ki-dee, who called himself the Contrary Warrior. Unpredictable men could be dangerous.

But it was Medicine Flute who changed his thinking.

"Panther Clan, why do you fret so?" he said quietly so the rest couldn't hear. "Why not champion this duel? If Big Tree kills Woman Face, all the better. If not, if Woman Face kills him, so what? We can form a new alliance with the next Comanche leader."

Wolf Who Hunts Smiling nodded. "I have ears for this." He turned to face his cousin, his spirited little paint prancing first left, then right. After all, it was Black Elk himself who had said that no red man on the plains could outride Big Tree.

Wolf Who Hunts Smiling met Black Elk's eyes. He nodded once.

Black Elk turned his pony to address Touch the Sky.

"Do you accept the challenge? I cannot and will not order you to do it."

"Tell me, war leader. Would you do it?" Touch the Sky demanded.

Fire sparked in Black Elk's eyes. He scowled fiercely, not hesitating a heartbeat. "If I were the buck he challenged, yes, I would. I would expect to die, of course, for I have watched this Big Tree ride and fight. Indeed, he sent me and my men scrambling for cover. But I fear no man."

"Brother," Little Horse said in a voice just above a whisper, "leave this challenge alone. Big Tree has deliberately limited the fight to riding skills, and you know no man has a chance against him on that score. What good is it to die by his terms? Better to live by yours."

"Good counsel, brother," Touch the Sky said calmly. "As always. You always speak straight arrow to me. Sadly, I do not listen as often as I should."

Touch the Sky faced Black Elk. Then he shared a long glance between Medicine Flute and Wolf Who Hunts Smiling. A sudden impulse made him grin at them and inject bantering sarcasm into his tone.

"Though I know it will break many hearts to see me dead, tell Big Tree I accept his challenge."

Chapter Twelve

After accepting Big Tree's challenge, Touch the Sky took on a different status among his comrades in the Cheyenne war party. He was still alive, yet, in the eyes of most, as good as dead.

Few disputed that he was the best warrior to send out. True, Black Elk and a few others were more experienced riders, and still others had the necessary courage and fighting spirit. But Touch the Sky was that rare warrior whose cool cunning increased with the desperation of his plight. He could unleash a mad war whoop and charge with the best of them, and yet, he was just as likely to win a fight by burying his enemies in a rock slide or by disguising a naked white boy as an evil spirit.

Still, this time, he was up against a foe the likes of whom he had never met before. To the Cheyennes, especially those who had seen him in action, this sneering Comanche in the tall shako hat was not a mere man, but some terrifying spawn of the Wendigo. And even those few skeptics who did not consider him in league with the Wendigo agreed he was the most dangerous mortal warrior on the plains.

For these reasons, all taunting and disparaging of Touch the Sky had ceased as if by silent order. Where he walked, braves stepped respectfully aside. Voices were not raised in his presence. Even his worst enemies recognized this new respect and left their foe alone. They simply avoided his eyes, as if he were already dead.

Little Horse had tried in vain to stop his friend. But once the challenge was accepted, he reacted as a warrior must. He assumed victory was theirs to earn if they acted like men.

"Brother," he said, early on the morning appointed for the crucial contest, "will you ride your bay? The new mare you acquired from Chief True Bow's Sioux is powerful. She snorts pure fire! But you are still training her. The bay is well trained, and she knows your touch."

Touch the Sky had been wrestling with that same question. The two Cheyennes were watching Touch the Sky's ponies graze with the rest in a hastily strung rope corral. To avoid surprise moves by either war party, both groups had agreed to meet in the wide-open flatland near the melon-shaped Pueblo Mountains.

"The bay knows my touch, and I hers," Touch the Sky agreed. He could pick the bay out easily by the pure white blaze on her forehead. "But the mare, her wild blood is still running closer to the surface. She trembles with the urge to break free and soar."

Little Horse was cautious. "Yes, clearly. And for this very reason, you will find her less predictable."

Touch the Sky nodded. "But so will Big Tree."

Little Horse narrowed his eyes, studying his friend closely.

"Sometimes," he said slowly, "a man gets a feeling that runs against the grain of good sense. My uncle, Roaring Bear of the Crooked Lance Clan, fought at Washita Creek. When a fellow warrior lost all his weapons, my uncle chose to give him his good new rifle instead of his pistol.

"His clan brothers chided him, saying he had sacrificed a good pony for a lame dog. But that night, they were attacked in their sleep. My uncle had his pistol to hand and killed a blue blouse only a heartbeat before he himself would have died. Never could he have fired his rifle so quickly."

Little Horse was thoughtful, watching the white mare impatiently stamp in protest at the pesky flies. "Ride her then, brother, if you have a feeling."

Tangle Hair had joined them. Cheyenne warriors were allowed great leeway in the matter of choosing weapons. He knew that Touch the Sky did not normally carry a war club. But all of the Bow String troopers did, and now Tangle Hair held out his. Not the fearsome, solid-stone skull cracker of Comanche fame—this

133

was a wooden mallet carved from solid oak. The striking surfaces were cruelly tapered to concentrate and focus the power of the blow. It was carved with the magic totems of Tangle Hair's clan.

"It has killed before," Tangle Hair said solemnly as he handed it over.

By now Touch the Sky had learned the ritual when accepting a borrowed weapon.

"And it will kill again," he promised just as solemnly when he accepted it.

The war clubs would be a roughly even match. As for the second weapon permitted by Big Tree's challenge—lances—here Touch the Sky was at a clear disadvantage. The Cheyennes, valuing mobility in battle above all else, opted for lighter weapons. This one was made from sturdy but lightweight osage wood, tipped with sharp flint. Comanche lances, in contrast, were longer, made of heavier wood and tipped with heavy stone heads chiseled to lethal points.

"He will have the reach on you," Little Horse said, watching his friend carefully examine his red-streamered lance for weak spots. "Best have one of your famous tricks to hand, brother."

Even as he finished speaking, the shout was taken up from those on the south flank of camp. The cry was repeated over and over, a menacing refrain:

"Here come the Comanches!"

Big Tree's superbly muscled chestnut with the stocking feet was the strongest, swiftest pony on the Comanche string. As was customary in such a duel, Big Tree had stripped off his saddle to reduce weight and targets—a good hit to the saddle could throw a man from his mount.

Touch the Sky, too, had left his blanket and rope rigging off his mare. Both braves would ride bareback, holding onto and directing the pony with their tight-gripping legs.

The Comanches lined up on one flank of a huge clearing, the Cheyennes on another. All were armed, their weapons at the ready. Insults were freely exchanged, though few understood what their enemies said.

"Look!" the Comanche named Rain in His Face shouted out. "These northerners have all cropped their hair off for their dead! How noble! They make shows of grief like women! No doubt they cried like puling babies over their dead ponies."

"Look here, brothers!" the Cheyenne named Snake Eater countered. "These Comanches mate with dogs. See their plug-ugly faces, how the nose and mouth are so like a snout? Indeed, they lick their own crotches and eat their own droppings!"

Stone Club had been chosen as the Comanche referee; Black Elk as the Cheyenne's. The two braves met in midclearing, on foot and unarmed. Touch the Sky and Big Tree joined them for the drawing of the reeds. Touch the Sky drew the short reed—meaning Big Tree got to choose the direction from which he would ride.

"I have nothing to fear from this Cheyenne. So I will ride into the sun," he announced in English.

When Wolf Who Hunts Smiling translated this, many of the Cheyenne warriors were puzzled. Why would the fierce warrior wish to have the sun facing him, rather than in his opponent's eyes? This was indeed a brave show of contempt.

Big Tree lowered his voice, still speaking in English. His eyes mocking Touch the Sky, he addressed a final comment to his enemy.

"Know this, haughty one! They say you are a shaman. And perhaps they say straight, for I am staring now at the wound that should have killed you. But all your medicine could not keep me from bulling your honey-skinned woman when she was my prisoner in Blanco Canyon. And she enjoyed it, Cheyenne! She howled like a hot coyote and told me she had never been mounted by a man until she had a Comanche. Think, in these final moments left before I kill you, of me topping her."

Touch the Sky was beyond rising to such obvious bait.

"Certainly I can see you rutting on a pig, for such are your own filthy women," he replied. "Though everyone knows that the Comanche men are more likely to bull each other in their drunkenness. Indeed, the men take turns playing the squaw for each other."

This was a capital hit, and for a moment rage flashed in Big Tree's eyes. But he caught himself in time and only grinned. As he turned to take up his position, he spoke almost fondly.

"You are a man among men, with no cowardly bones in your body. I am going to enjoy killing you, tall Cheyenne."

The mare felt like a tightly coiled spring under him as Touch the Sky trotted her to his starting point and turned her to face his opponent.

The sun was well up behind him, casting his slanting shadow before him. Still he was puzzled. Why had Big Tree opted to face the sun? Touch the Sky did not believe it was merely a gesture of contempt. It was a sacred Comanche habit to attack from out of the sun.

But he had no luxury for examining the motivations of his enemy. The mare, sensing excitement in the air, was rebellious and required constant attention to keep her in position. She bucked several times, sidestepped, and hopped before settling down.

When the riders were set, lances balanced on their thighs, Black Elk suddenly thrust his arms into the sky. With a whoop, both riders were off.

Divots of dirt were flung into the air by the ponies' hooves; both riders gripped hard with their thighs and raised their lances and shields. Touch the Sky spotted sudden bursts of light, then abruptly squinted when blinding flashes forced him to avert his face. His pony, too, faltered, and Touch the Sky suddenly understood why Big Tree had chosen to face the sun. The fragments of mirror embedded in his shield were blinding the Cheyenne and his pony!

The two warriors thundered closer to each other, Touch the Sky desperately trying to orient himself in the brief pauses when the reflection missed his eyes. He saw Big Tree grinning behind the heavy stone point of his lance. When they were almost upon each other, Touch the Sky made his move.

He shifted right and forward, lying low over the pony's neck. This threw the sun out of his eyes. Big Tree's first lance thrust missed him by inches. Touch the Sky, off balance, only managed to strike his enemy's shield a glancing blow. Then, a heartbeat later, they had passed each other and were turning for the next attempt.

Now Touch the Sky rode into the sun, and Big Tree could not use his mirror fragments. Touch the Sky had been fighting his pony to control her. Now, on an impulse, he decided to give the feisty little mare her head.

Big Tree, still grinning, bounced with perilous ease atop his chestnut. Again he raised his lance, preparing to skewer the tall Cheyenne. The ponies drew closer, manes flying. Big Tree drew his arm back, ready to strike.

But now Touch the Sky's white mare showed her wildness.

With a hard shudder, she deliberately threw herself against the chestnut, taking a good nip out of its flank. The impact made the beast stumble, and Big Tree had to scramble wildly for a hold.

A cheer rose from the Cheyennes. Surely the Comanche was doomed now!

Spirit Path

But in an amazing show of balance and strength, man and horse avoided going down. And now Touch the Sky was turning for the third pass.

Again these two implacable foes bore down on each other; again Touch the Sky had to keep glancing aside as mirror flashes blinded him. Before he even had time to think, Big Tree's lance point was flying straight at his heart.

In a skillful move, Touch the Sky got his lance up in time to parry the blow. Then, tragedy. As Touch the Sky's parry knocked Big Tree's lance aside, the tip of his own lance punched into the side of his pony. She shuddered once, then blew pink foam from her punctured lung. The mare slowed to a walk, staggered, and collapsed under him. Suddenly, Touch the Sky was standing on the ground beside his dying pony, and Big Tree whirled around to deliver the death blow.

The Comanche had tossed aside his lance in favor of his stone skull cracker. The ground thundered and vibrated as he closed the distance, sure of the kill this time. A cheer rose from the Comanche spectators as they sniffed blood in the wind.

Best have one of your famous tricks to hand, brother.

Little Horse's words taunted Touch the Sky. He had no medicine to help him. Only the words of old Arrow Keeper. During the short white days of the cold moons, as they huddled near the fire pit in the old shaman's tipi, Arrow Keeper had told his young apprentice many stories about famous Cheyenne battles. One of those stories was about the Cheyenne warrior named Running Antelope—the same warrior who Arrow Keeper claimed was Touch the Sky's father.

This warrior, Arrow Keeper had claimed, once faced a mounted Ute warrior on foot and brought his horse down with a daring move invented by Cheyenne warriors in the days before they had acquired horses to fight their mounted enemies.

Big Tree bore closer, his skull cracker raised high. He was leaning far out from his pony, balanced for the blow that would send Touch the Sky across the great divide. Now the Comanches were cheering wildly, knowing it was only a matter of time before the unmounted Cheyenne dog was brained.

The pony was nearly upon him when Touch the Sky feinted to the left. But he checked his movement and dropped to the right, spinning his body as he fell.

Timing was everything, and Touch the Sky had timed it perfectly.

As the chestnut flashed past, and the skull cracker whipped by his head so close that Touch the Sky felt the wind from it, he wrapped his body hard around the pony's left foreleg.

For a moment his grip was precarious and he was almost thrown free. Then he found purchase and clung on for dear life, feeling the powerful pony shudder, then trip. Touch the Sky knew it might well fall on him, crushing him to death, but he had no other choice.

Spirit Path

The chestnut crashed hard to the ground, tossing Touch the Sky in a hard tumble across the open field. And the last thing the Cheyenne saw was Big Tree crashing with his pony. Then the Cheyenne's head struck a rock hard, and Touch the Sky's world shut down to darkness.

Chapter Thirteen

Both groups, Cheyenne and Comanche, had fallen silent at this unexpected outcome. The two warriors now lay less than a stone's throw apart, and for all anyone knew, both were dead.

On the Cheyenne side, Little Horse and Tangle Hair had started to run forward to check on Touch the Sky. On the Comanche side, likewise, braves started out to check on their fallen leader. But Black Elk and Stone Club quickly ordered them back. The fight was not over until they declared it so.

On the Cheyenne side, even Touch the Sky's enemies were clearly impressed by the amazing tactic he had just employed to bring down Big Tree's horse. Neither luck nor magic had anything to do with it. The courageous, agile brave had timed his move perfectly and shown the fighting courage of a she-bear defending her cubs.

Even the Comanches—who measured all men by their fighting skill—showed a certain respect in their faces. Big Tree had done well, they all agreed, and need not feel shame that he was on the ground. But this tall, brazen Cheyenne, clearly he was the victor—if he were still alive.

At almost the same moment, both men moved. And then all the spectators realized that whoever got up first would surely kill the other.

"Get up, Cheyenne!" Little Horse urged, his face grim and tense. "Stand up, buck! Today is not a good day to die."

"Quickly," Tangle Hair said. "Quickly, Touch the Sky! Stand and live!"

A moment later, as if obeying them, Touch the Sky slowly sat up and shook his head to clear it.

A mighty cheer rose from the Cheyenne side. Even those who had lately turned against the tall young buck—with the exception of Wolf Who Hunts Smiling, Medicine Flute, and a few of the Bull Whip troopers—showed loyalty to their tribe and pride in this *Shaiyena* victory.

Touch the Sky saw the dead mare, his lance still protruding from her bloody chest. And he saw Big Tree lying nearby, out cold but still breathing.

"Kill him, Touch the Sky!" a Cheyenne shouted. Several others chorused support.

"Remember the herd guards, Touch the Sky! This one led their slaughter. Kill him!"

Tangle Hair's war club was still lashed to Touch the Sky's legging sash. Touch the Sky untied the rawhide whang securing it. He felt the solid osage wood filling his grip as he slowly stood up and crossed to the supine Comanche.

By the rules of the fight, Touch the Sky was permitted a kill, so long as it was done with one of the weapons agreed upon. He assumed a wide stance over his downed foe and raised the club high, preparing to brain him.

He hesitated, some inner revulsion filling him. This was not a kill, he thought. It was simply slaughter, as one might thump a half-dead rabbit against a tree to finish it off.

"Kill him, Touch the Sky! Kill the Comanche dog!"

"This pig's afterbirth killed our elders and children and kidnapped our people. Kill him!"

Touch the Sky's muscles trembled. Still the revulsion filled him, for a true warrior disdained to kill a sleeping or unconscious foe.

He glanced over at his people. His eyes met Little Horse's. And quite clearly, Little Horse shook his head no. For in that moment, he, too, realized the same truth Arrow Keeper had spoken all along. Touch the Sky was marked out for a special destiny. He was bound by a higher code than most others. The words of old Arrow Keeper came back now to both of the youths, guiding their decision: *If gold will rust, what then will iron do?*

Touch the Sky was meant to someday lead the entire Cheyenne nation. The code of the warrior required more than courage and skill at killing. It also required magnanimity and compassion. It mattered not who Big Tree was. He was on the ground, defeated, and no more violence was required.

There was yet another consideration. Touch the Sky carefully gauged the mood of the Comanche warriors. Their weapons were to hand—was a bloody battle guaranteed the moment Touch the Sky killed Big Tree? So long as there was no loss of honor in it, Touch the Sky wanted to spare his comrades from a fight. If they must die, let it be a tribal decision, not because of his actions. A leader's first obligation was the welfare of his men.

A few of his own people hissed when Touch the Sky dropped the war club to the ground. But others, including Little Horse and Tangle Hair, looked at him with open admiration.

Touch the Sky faced the Comanches. He addressed them in English while a Comanche who spoke that language translated.

"I have fought your best warrior. Now here I stand, a living man. In the name of my tribe, I will accept our ponies back and call that debt settled. You may take this one"—he nodded toward the prone Comanche—"with you.

"Only, know this. I have no authority to speak for my entire tribe or to cancel other debts. Our guards were slain, and their ghosts cry out for bloody revenge! This is not a permanent peace I propose now, only a ceasing of present hostilities. What say you?"

There was a long pause while the Comanches discussed this thorny matter. It was Rain in His Face who finally answered.

"Your terms are accepted, Bear Caller! We saw you fight today, and you are a man to be respected. When our leader once again has sap flowing in him, we will send a word-bringer to announce the time and place to surrender the ponies."

This was well-spoken. Both braves had been careful to save face for the other tribe. Since this was ultimately a matter for his war leader to decide, Touch the Sky looked to Black Elk. This fierce warrior nodded once. Despite his hatred for Touch the Sky, Black Elk knew that the youth had acted and spoken like a straight-arrow Cheyenne.

Touch the Sky also noticed a look of relief pass over Wolf Who Hunts Smiling's face. Obviously, he did not want Big Tree killed. That would cost him his newest ally, Touch the Sky thought bitterly.

Clearly, he told himself, despite his narrow escape today, the trouble was far from over.

Wolf Who Hunts Smiling was worried.

His conspiracy with Medicine Flute had been working well. Slowly, steadily, they had chipped away at Touch the Sky's credibility, weakening his position in the tribe. And now this victory over Big Tree threatened to undo all their careful work.

"Brother," he said to Medicine Flute, "everywhere I turn, the talk is all about how White Man Runs Him brought down a charging pony. We can cast shadows over his medicine. But his skill as a warrior is there for all to see."

Medicine Flute nodded, his heavy-lidded gaze making him appear drowsy. The two braves had slipped away from the trail camp to plot their newest strategy.

"It was impressive," Medicine Flute said. "He is a warrior to reckon with. But did you notice how his face showed his loathing when it came time to kill Big Tree?"

"I have ears for this. We think as one, brother. Neither of us would have hesitated to smash an unconscious enemy's skull, though indeed I would have this Big Tree live. A leader of men cannot harbor a soft place in his heart like a woman."

"What can we do now? For, brother, truly, comets do not streak across the heavens often enough to suit our plans."

"No," Wolf Who Hunts Smiling agreed, "they do not. But as usual, I have an idea. And do not forget. We still do not have our pony herd back. Many things may still happen."

Wolf Who Hunts Smiling slipped a few fingers into his parfleche. They emerged holding a small, brightly polished bloodstone. A hole had been pierced into it and a rawhide thong strung through it.

"White Man Runs Him removed the rigging from his horse before the fight. But he left the hackamore on. He carried it with him when he walked off the battlefield. Now it is on his bay.

"Take this. I will distract Woman Face and his companions while you slip in among the ponies and tie this to his hackamore."

Medicine Flute's heavy-lidded eyes widened with curiosity.

"Why, Panther Clan?"

Wolf Who Hunts Smiling grinned. "You will see, all in good time. Just agree with whatever I say, medicine man."

"Brother," Little Horse said, "now I see that your feeling about riding the white mare was just. Big Tree would have skewered you on that second pass, had your pony not attacked his chestnut."

Touch the Sky nodded. "She saved my life, yet I could not save hers."

"She died hard," Tangle Hair agreed. "But you did not kill her, Cheyenne."

"Sadly," Touch the Sky said, "I feel the victory only means more trouble from Big Tree. He is not one to calmly brook defeat."

"Do you think he will return our ponies?" Little Horse said.

Touch the Sky shook his head. "I cannot read the trail of his thoughts. He has treachery in his eyes. And much depends on his silent partner, Wolf Who Hunts Smiling."

The three braves were filing arrow points in the center of the temporary trail camp. All around them, warriors were at work on their weapons and battle rigs. Still, the Comanche word-bringer had not arrived with news about the return of the ponies.

A cooking fire blazed in the middle of camp. The hindquarters of an antelope were roasting over it on a spit. Touch the Sky saw Wolf Who Hunts Smiling walk close to the fire.

Wolf Who Hunts Smiling's hand flicked out quick as a snake and tossed something bright into the flames. A moment later, gunshots rang out and every brave scrambled for cover.

Medicine Flute worked quickly in the confusion. He crossed to the tethered ponies, picked out Touch the Sky's buffalo-hair bridle, and quickly tied the bloodstone to it. He slipped away again, unobserved.

"Brothers!" Wolf Who Hunts Smiling shouted even as Black Elk began barking orders to form a defensive perimeter. "False alarm! Rest easy! My shot pouch rolled too close to the fire and some primer caps went off."

"Such carelessness, cousin," Black Elk said sternly, "is the mark of a green warrior."

Wolf Who Hunts Smiling nodded, his face contrite. But clearly he had only been waiting to address the entire camp. Now was his chance, while he had their attention.

"Brothers, hear me. Medicine Flute has asked me to be silent about a thing. He is modest and desires no credit. But I would speak it."

"We are not coy maidens in their sewing lodge," Black Elk said impatiently. "Speak this thing or hold your tongue."

"Earlier, we all watched White Man Runs Him—"

"His name is Touch the Sky," Little Horse cut in hotly, "a name he lived up to again today. If any brave deserves the name of traitor, Panther Clan, it is you."

Rage smoldered in Wolf Who Hunts Smiling's eyes. But he only smiled mockingly, a smile that promised trouble to come.

"Earlier we all watched Touch the Sky perform amazing feats. Indeed, his skill seemed almost supernatural. And I say it was. For Medicine Flute placed a powerful magic talisman on his pony's hackamore. He blessed it with his strongest medicine."

"There is no talisman on my bridle," Touch the Sky retorted. "I inspected it before the fight."

"Inspect it now, Woman Fa—Cheyenne! I tell you it is there. I caught Medicine Flute tying it on in secret before the fight."

Touch the Sky spoke quietly to Tangle Hair. This brave crossed toward the ponies.

"And tell us, Panther Clan," Touch the Sky said. "Since when has Medicine Flute begun worrying about my fate?"

"Mock, pretend shaman! He did this magnanimous act because he would protect any Cheyenne. He has no quarrel with you. You were riding into an impossible fight, and he did not wish to see you slaughtered. Also, the return of our ponies rested on the outcome of this battle."

Through all this, Medicine Flute sat unperturbed, playing his eerie music as if none of this concerned him. The rest had formed a circle.

They stared hard at Tangle Hair as he crossed back to the camp circle and held up a smooth bloodstone on a rawhide thong.

"This was indeed tied to your pony's hackamore," he said, confusion clear in his eyes.

Chapter Fourteen

At the first opportunity Wolf Who Hunts Smiling rode out, claiming he was on a scouting mission. But he knew the Comanche word-bringer named Stone Club, who like the Cheyenne spoke some English, would be lurking in the area.

Wolf Who Hunts Smiling made sure he had not been followed from camp. Then he tied a white truce flag to his bridle—the prearranged signal that it was safe for the Comanche to reveal himself.

The meeting took place in a sandy wash, sheltered from the eyes of any Cheyenne scouts or sentries. Wolf Who Hunts Smiling explained his latest plan carefully. When he finished speaking, Stone Club's eyes were bright with appreciative mirth.

"Big Tree will like this," he said, slowly nodding. "He lost face in the encounter with the tall one. This plan, it will gain him a fitting revenge. You are aptly named, Wolf Who Hunts Smiling. I see good days ahead for our two tribes now that you and Big Tree have shared a pipe."

"Men of force and action will do well in this rich land," Wolf Who Hunts Smiling said. "It is there for the taking, as the hair faces understand.

"But my people, led by compromising cowards and white men's dogs, hope to follow the peace road. They must be more like your tribe, who kill the paleface intruders and steal their goods at every opportunity. First we must kill or remove from power these pretend Indians who preach coexistence with hair faces."

"I have ears for this. We Comanche have earned the name of the Red Raiders of the Plains. We have killed more white settlers than any tribe. Especially have we slaughtered these bragging, swaggering Texans, whom we hate above all other white intruders.

"But truly, the paleface numbers are vast, as vast as the very plains they hope to conquer. You speak the straight word, Cheyenne. We red men must bury the hatchet, put our own battles behind us, and turn with a vengeance to the slaughter of these stinking foreigners."

Stone Club added a sly smile as he prepared to ride out. "And of course, while eliminating these whites and the Indians who play the dog for them, perhaps a few Indians will profit handsomely?"

Wolf Who Hunts Smiling matched his grin. "Our thoughts run one way, Red Raider. Perhaps I would have been happy as a Comanche."

Stone Club nodded. "You would make a fine Quohada! You are brazen and crafty and make the he-bear talk with the best. I will take your message to Big Tree. And count upon it, he will approve this plan."

Big Tree had indeed lost face in the encounter with the tall Cheyenne warrior who rode the pure white pony.

True, the Comanche had not been seriously hurt. Nor had the battle been an outright victory for the Cheyenne. After all, Touch the Sky had been knocked to the ground first, and his pony had been killed.

But unknowingly, the Cheyenne had humiliated Big Tree by not killing him. To many of the Comanche braves, the gesture of sparing his life was also a gesture of contempt. It suggested that Big Tree was too worthless to bother killing, as one might leave a coward to wallow in his own disgrace.

Big Tree had sent a word-bringer to announce the time and place for returning the ponies. But in fact, he had no plans to keep his word. Instead, he had intended to herd them fast toward the Blanco Canyon, the nearly impregnable Comanche stronghold in the middle of the burning Staked Plain.

Now, however, he listened with great interest as Stone Club explained the latest plan.

"It is simple," the brave said. "We are to drive

the ponies to the designated spot as you promised. Then, in an apparently surprise move, we are to form a skirmish line and attack. At this point, the Cheyenne called Medicine Flute will ride forward and play his magic flute.

"Wolf Who Hunts Smiling has spread the word among his brothers that his music can frighten off an enemy. At the first notes, our warriors are to shriek, as if in mortal terror, then flee."

Big Tree thought about this. "But we would lose the ponies?"

Stone Club nodded. "We would. But the encounter will be bloodless for us, yet it will finally turn the Cheyennes against this Touch the Sky. This would place Medicine Flute in a special position of power. And we will then profit much more handsomely later."

Big Tree was ironic enough to appreciate all this. For of course, once Medicine Flute rose to power, so would Wolf Who Hunts Smiling. But Big Tree was no fool. This Wolf Who Hunts Smiling, he had no intention of sharing any wealth or power with other leaders. He would use them so long as they were helpful, then kill them. For after all, this was what Big Tree himself would do.

"Still," he said, musing out loud, "according to this plan, the tall shaman would still be alive."

"He would be," Stone Club agreed, watching his leader's weather-seamed face shrewdly. For though Stone Club had spoken conciliatory words to Wolf Who Hunts Smiling, he knew his leader would have his own plans.

Big Tree said, "If we must sacrifice the ponies, we should at least have the satisfaction of killing the tall one and a few more Cheyennes."

The Comanche leader made up his mind. "Tell Wolf Who Hunts Smiling that I agree to his plan. But now have ears, Quohada, for we Comanches will add a surprise of our own."

Touch the Sky knew some serious treachery was afoot.

A Comanche word-bringer had arrived with news from Big Tree. As promised, the Cheyenne pony herd would be returned. The exchange was due to take place in one sleep, on the same wide-open flat near the Pueblo Mountains where the fateful duel had taken place.

But Touch the Sky knew better. Long ago Arrow Keeper had assured him there was no more despicable and untrustworthy tribe in the red nations than the Comanches. Even the Pawnee did not surpass them in cunning and deceit and sheer, bloodthirsty evil. Clearly, trouble was in the wind.

Black Elk, as war leader, was no fool either. He called an informal outdoor council on the night before the exchange was set.

"Brothers, if all goes well we will have our ponies back before the next appearance of the Always Star. I do not think the cricket-eating Comanches are keen for a fight with us. Our fathers and uncles defeated them at Wolf Creek in the bloodiest battle they have ever seen.

"And yet, they are fully capable of some

deceit. Their fighting style has been shaped by long contact with the barbarous Spaniards. More than one of their victims has died in his sleep after being invited into their camp for food and drink. Watch their eyes closely, keep your best weapon to hand, and do not turn your back on them."

"Your words are well-spoken," Chief Gray Thunder said. "What is said of the Apaches is equally true of the Comanches. 'When you can see them, be careful. When you cannot see them, be even more careful.'"

Wolf Who Hunts Smiling rose to speak. "Brothers! Black Elk and our chief have spoken wise words we may pick up and examine. Medicine Flute and I have discussed this thing. He agrees that some danger looms. Therefore, he has strong medicine planned against our enemy."

Touch the Sky, Little Horse, and Tangle Hair all exchanged glances in the flickering light of the campfire. Not all had been completely convinced by the talisman found tied to Touch the Sky's hackamore. But this, added to the miracle of the burning star and his two visions, had many convinced that Medicine Flute was a straight-arrow shaman.

Even now, Medicine Flute sat aloof and drowsy eyed, his leg-bone flute silent in his lap. He had only reluctantly stopped playing, in recognition of the council. His eyes met Touch the Sky's for a moment, mocking him.

"What manner of strong medicine, cousin?" Black Elk said.

157

"You have been listening to it for many sleeps now. Many in the tribe have foolishly complained of the music produced by his bone flute. And yet, why do you think he made that instrument from the bone of a defeated enemy? The answer is simple. Because the notes it produces are powerful medicine against any enemy."

Black Elk's fierce scowl took on a thoughtful cast. He knew, of course, that his cousin and Medicine Flute had cleverly been playing the fox to discredit Touch the Sky. And Black Elk approved of it because he hated this squaw-stealing dog who would put on the old moccasin by bulling his Honey Eater. But what was Wolf Who Hunts Smiling up to now? This leg-bone flute, truly its music was odd and unnerving. Was there medicine to it? More likely, his cousin was simply counting on the Comanches not to attack.

"This night," Wolf Who Hunts Smiling continued, "Medicine Flute will separate himself and perform a sweat-lodge ceremony. He will pray and make offerings to the High Holy Ones. And then, if trouble takes us by the tail tomorrow, his flute will save us. For played on the battlefield, it will scatter an enemy as surely as shotgun pellets scatter crows."

This claim caused a low hum of conversation around the fire. Touch the Sky rose.

"Brothers! Gray Thunder has reminded me of my promise not to publicly accuse Wolf Who Hunts Smiling of grazing with our enemy. I will respect my chief on that score and hold my tongue. I have only this to say.

"Earlier, I saw Wolf Who Hunts Smiling deliberately throw something into the fire. The objects were small and bright, like primer caps. Moments later we were all distracted by what we thought was gunfire. And then, only behold! Suddenly a talisman appears on my horse. Warriors, draw your own conclusions. I say only this. Nothing can destroy a tribe more quickly than treachery from within."

"I agree," Wolf Who Hunts Smiling shot back. "And I say only this. I have never drunk strong water with paleface dogs. I have never deserted my tribe during danger to go fight white men's battles. I did not collaborate with white miners to build a road for the iron horse across our ancient homeland. I have never scattered the buffalo herds with my white man's stink.

"Who is the traitor here? A straight-arrow Cheyenne whose father was killed by blue-bloused devils, or a pretend Cheyenne who arrived among us wearing shoes and offering his hand for us to shake?"

Touch the Sky leveled a murderous stare at his enemy. "Strut and throw your arms about. You are like the white liars who leap on tree stumps to scream their untruths. Only my promise to Gray Thunder forces me to bite back a reply about traitors. I say this again, Panther Clan. The time is fast approaching when I am going to kill you."

Later that night many watched, respectfully curious, as Medicine Flute fashioned a sweat

159

lodge from hides draped over a bent-branch frame. He heated a circle of rocks to a red glow, then poured water on them. Late into the night, while steam billowed from the makeshift lodge, he chanted and prayed and played his disturbing music.

Touch the Sky, in contrast, quietly separated himself from the rest. He found a little copse where pinon trees grew close, forming a little covered shelter. He ensconced himself within. Long into the night, as the noises from camp settled into slumber, he lay wide awake.

For every battle road, Arrow Keeper had once told him, *there is a spirit road*.

Touch the Sky did not chant. He did not make offerings or shake snake teeth in a gourd. He merely lay quietly, stopping all conscious thought and attending, instead, to the language of his senses. Thus, Arrow Keeper had assured him, could the true visionary reach the upward path of the Spirit Way.

When his guiding vision finally arrived, it was neither very dramatic nor very detailed. He simply saw himself, riding alone in front of the rest of his companions. He carried no weapons, performed no amazing riding tricks. In fact, only one detail was out of the ordinary. Instead of being stripped to his clout for battle, as Cheyennes did, he wore the beautiful mountain lion skin Arrow Keeper had once given him.

It was a paltry revelation. So little, in fact, that he wondered if it had truly been a vision.

But he decided to act on faith and assume it was.

Tomorrow, against the most treacherous enemy of the *Shaiyena* people, he would ride unarmed into the teeth of his foes.

Chapter Fifteen

"Brother," Medicine Flute said, a nervous edge to his voice, "a thing troubles me."

He and Wolf Who Hunts Smiling stood a little way off from the rest, rigging their ponies. This was the day that Big Tree had named for the return of the ponies. Throughout camp, a grim sense of purpose could be felt. Braves attended to their weapons and applied their battle paint. They carefully rigged their ponies for possible combat, securing weapons and shields so they would be ready to hand in the heat of battle.

Wolf Who Hunts Smiling frowned impatiently. The normally imperturbable Medicine Flute showed signs of nervous tension now that the confrontation approached.

"Buck," he said, "I am not skilled in divination. Either speak this thing or get on with your preparations."

"These Comanches, they are no braves to fool with. And Big Tree, his cunning would make a fox blush."

Wolf Who Hunts Smiling shrugged. "So? Everyone knows this."

"But, brother, your plan would have me ride out ahead armed only with my flute, since I cannot play it and wield a weapon. What if these marauders have deceit in their sashes? I will be among the first to fall."

"And what of that? You will thus die the glorious death of a warrior. Do you think I will be riding at the rear? Would you rather die in your tipi like some ancient squaw with drool on her chin?"

In fact, Medicine Flute did hope to die of old age in his tipi. But the men of Wolf Who Hunts Smiling's Panther Clan would tolerate no fainthearted braves. They placed great importance on never showing fear in their voices or faces. Either a man was a stout warrior or he was a woman. A young man of the Panther Clan had once fled from a battle. After that, he was forced to wear a dress and wait on the men until, in mortal shame, he fell on his own knife.

"I am not afraid of death," Medicine Flute lied. "But like you, I have great ambition. I wish to taste the fruits of power before I cross over. If I die now, all of our careful scheming comes to naught, a thing of smoke. And, buck, if I die, you lose your best chance for doing the hurt dance on Woman Face."

These words flew straight arrow and struck the sarcasm from Wolf Who Hunts Smiling's manner.

"Well said, brother. Only, do not shed so much brain sweat worrying about Big Tree. True it is, he is a treacherous Comanche. But he, too, thirsts for power as we do. However, you are right, we have no assurance he will not outfox us. Therefore, know this. I will ride beside you, close as your very shadow, and protect you with my life. You know how I fight."

"Like ten men," Medicine Flute said, genuinely reassured. Many considered Wolf Who Hunts Smiling the best warrior in the tribe—though just as many gave the nod to Touch the Sky.

As for Wolf Who Hunts Smiling, he was less worried about Big Tree than he was about his cousin Black Elk. Once Medicine Flute's playing scattered the Comanches, he would again suspect Wolf Who Hunts Smiling of grazing with their enemy. But his joy at seeing Touch the Sky humiliated would make him less eager to cry traitor.

And Wolf Who Hunts Smiling already had his strategy ready. He would remind his cousin that the Comanches, too, were superstitious— witness the roadrunner skins tied to the tails of their ponies for good luck. Perhaps, he would argue to his cousin, the leg-bone flute might actually frighten them. After all, Woman Face had once sent the entire Pawnee tribe running merely by painting a naked white boy and telling him to act insane.

Besides, Black Elk was clearly confused on the question of medicine. He still believed things Wolf Who Hunts Smiling had rejected in his thirst for power. He might well end up believing in the medicine flute—even better for Wolf Who Hunts Smiling's plans.

"If Big Tree does have some tricks in his sash," Wolf Who Hunts Smiling added, "know this. In the heat of battle, it is not uncommon for warriors to accidentally kill their own men."

Medicine Flute watched his companion's wily, furtive face closely. "You mean Touch the Sky?"

"Who else, buck? For I have made up my mind. If the Comanches flee when you start playing your flute, as agreed, White Man Runs Him will lose the last of his credibility. If they outfox us and attack, I will kill him in the confusion. Either way, after this day he will sleep with the worms."

"Brother," Little Horse said, watching Wolf Who Hunts Smiling and Medicine Flute confer, "I am no more of a shaman than Medicine Flute. But I clearly see trouble preparing to rear its ugly head."

"Indeed, brother. It needs no strong medicine to read such sign as they make."

Touch the Sky, Little Horse, and Tangle Hair were making their final preparations. Using claybank paint, they smeared their faces red, yellow, and black, the traditional Cheyenne battle colors. Bow strings had been checked,

165

rifles cleaned, and shields prepared.

"Cheyenne," Tangle Hair said to Touch the Sky, "you are painted, and I see that you plan to wear the fine mountain lion skin you wear for the Sun Dance. But why are you not attending to your weapons?"

"I am wearing my weapons, buck."

Confused, Tangle Hair looked to see if a knife or pistol were tucked behind the skin. "Then you have made them invisible, brother."

But Little Horse, who knew Touch the Sky better than anyone else in the tribe knew him, understood immediately. This had to do with the vision Touch the Sky had sought last night. However, Indians carefully skirted too much direct talk about holy matters. Things of the spirit were private and to be respected.

"Know this much," Little Horse said to Tangle Hair, "and then let it alone. The hand of the Good Supernatural is in this thing. Count upon it, no brave riding out today goes better armed than Touch the Sky."

Understanding glimmered in Tangle Hair's eyes, and he fell respectfully silent. But secretly, Touch the Sky wished he had as much confidence as Little Horse. For even now the words of old Arrow Keeper drifted back from the hinterland of memory:

Be warned. A medicine vision can be either a revelation or a curse. An enemy's bad medicine may place a false vision over our eyes, and we may act upon it, aiding our enemies and destroying those whom we seek to help.

Spirit Path

*   *   *

The Cheyenne warriors rode out in a double column, singing their battle songs.

Black Elk led one column, his cousin Wolf Who Hunts Smiling the other, Medicine Flute close at his side. The day was clear, a bright yellow ball of sun blazing from a sky of deep, bottomless blue except for a few puffy white clouds out over the horizon. In the distance, the Pueblo Mountains pushed their round humps into the soft belly of the sky.

Touch the Sky spotted the dust haze even before they reached the vast, open field where he had recently battled Big Tree. The cry went up throughout the ranks.

"Here come our ponies!"

"See them?"

"There is our herd!"

At least Big Tree planned to show up. It just might be possible, Touch the Sky told himself, that Big Tree would return the herd. Yet, his shaman's sense told him otherwise and never had he known it to steer him wrong.

His powerful little bay, too, sensed some excitement in the wind. Several times Touch the Sky was forced to pull hard on her hackamore to bring her back into line.

"Look here," the Bull Whip trooper named Snake Eater called out to his companions, nodding toward Touch the Sky. "He has dressed in a fine skin, but carries no weapon. Like the Crow warriors who fuss like women over their hair, he cares more about his looks than his manhood."

"Would you care to bridge the gap, Bull Whip," Touch the Sky replied calmly enough, "and see if I have my manhood with me?"

Snake Eater wisely declined this invitation. Now the ground thundered and trembled as the vast herd was driven closer by the skillful Comanches.

Black Elk halted his warriors on one flank of the grassy field.

"Live close to your weapons!" he called out. "Watch their eyes, and do not let them slip behind you. Whatever they say or do, no matter how friendly they may act, do not be foolish enough to let down your guard. These dogs will offer one hand to shake while the other guts you."

The herd thundered closer. Despite the mounting tension, Touch the Sky could not help marveling at the magnificent sight of so many fine ponies.

Then something began to trouble him. By now, the Comanches should have started ringing the herd to slow it. Instead, they were all riding behind the herd, driving it relentlessly on. A moment later a cool tickle moved up the bumps of his spine as he realized that Big Tree meant to overrun them with the charging herd!

"Black Elk!" he shouted. "They mean to trample us!"

And instantly Black Elk, too, saw the plan. Quickly, he formed the narrow columns into one single line stretching across the field.

"Charge the ponies!" he screamed. "Turn

them to the right flank and expose the enemy!"

"Hi-ya, hii-ya!"

Loosing their fierce battle cry, firing their weapons into the air, and waving their streamered lances, the Cheyenne warriors rushed forward. The plan worked perfectly. The line angled so that the ponies veered to the right. And within moments the two tribes were charging each other in a classic plains battle formation.

Medicine Flute's normally heavy-lidded eyes were wide with fright. He started to follow the ponies, but Wolf Who Hunts Smiling caught his bridle.

"You white-livered coward! Put that bone to your lips and play or I will have your guts for garters."

"But Big Tree has decided to attack!"

"His plan failed, fool. Now he will have to keep his word. Ride forward and play or die on the spot!"

Caught between the sap and the bark, Medicine Flute did as ordered. He had played perhaps a dozen notes when a Comanche bullet shattered his flute, driving a jagged piece of it through his cheek.

A heartbeat later an arrow caught Snake Eater in the eye, sending him to the ground writhing in agony. Now the two bands were within easy range of bullets and arrows.

But Touch the Sky felt his mouth dry with fear when he realized most of the Comanche braves were armed with the new repeating rifles of the type used by white buffalo hunters. It would be a slaughter against the Cheyennes armed with single-shot percussion rifles.

"Save a place for me at the scalp dance tonight, brother!" he shouted to Little Horse, even as he jabbed his knees hard into the bay's flanks.

Now the tough little mustang showed her magnificent breeding as she surged ahead of the rest. Touch the Sky bent low over her neck and urged her on. Another Cheyenne flung his arms to the heavens and flew from his pony as a bullet struck him in his lights. But now the Comanche warriors had noticed Touch the Sky in his colorful skin, surging unarmed ahead of the rest.

Repeated flashes of light told Touch the Sky where Big Tree was, his mirror-speckled shield reflecting in the bright sun. Deliberately, Touch the Sky bore down on their best fighter.

Big Tree's two quivers were stuffed with new arrows. He grinned, ignoring the rifle in his scabbard, and reached back to grab a handful of arrows. This was going to be like shooting a prairie chicken.

"He is mine!" he shouted to his men.

The fool rode even closer. Big Tree had launched five arrows before the first one had found his target's range.

Still the tall Cheyenne charged closer.

Big Tree frowned, grabbed another handful of arrows, launched them with lightning rapidity. Pieces of Touch the Sky's kit and rigging flapped loose, his hackamore snapped, several arrows snagged in his doeskin leggings but never touched his flesh. Still he charged, so close now he could count the silver conchos on Big Tree's tall shako hat.

Big Tree's face went numb. He had fired at least 15 arrows!

By now the rest of the Comanches had noticed what was happening and halted their charge, shock and confusion distorting their faces. Little Horse surged closer. His revolving-barrel shotgun blasted, and the Comanche named Stone Club dropped from his pony, his face shredded to raw meat.

Tangle Hair's British trade rifle cracked, and the brave named Gall took a slug flush through the throat.

"Kill him!" Big Tree shouted to his men as Touch the Sky was on the verge of overriding him.

A score of Comanche weapons opened up at almost point-blank range. Bullets and arrows fanned Touch the Sky's locks back off his forehead, hummed like angry hornets around his ears, and shredded the rest of his rope rigging and demolished his kit.

Still, the tall, broad-shouldered Cheyenne rode closer, his face split by a mocking grin.

This finally unstrung the Comanche nerves completely. They did not wait for a command from Big Tree. As one, those who had not already fallen spun their mounts around and fled from this terrible big medicine, from this terrifying Cheyenne shaman.

It took most of the daylight remaining to round up the scattered ponies and group them in the field for the night. Black Elk sent out a small guard to make sure their enemy would not return, but no one really expected them to. Nor was one sign of them spotted.

The mission had ended perfectly. They had regained almost the entire herd, minus the few ponies sacrificed by the Comanches along the way. Just as important, they had killed a half-dozen Comanche braves, evening the score for the Cheyenne herd guards slaughtered when the ponies were taken.

An impromptu scalp dance was indeed held that night. The warriors danced fast and hard around a blazing fire, their knees kicking high while fellow Cheyennes kept time with sticks on a hollow log.

True, two braves had been killed, four others wounded including Medicine Flute. But all agreed that it was a light price to pay for this victory. And even Touch the Sky's enemies admitted he had saved them from disaster against so many repeating rifles.

"Medicine Flute," a brave called out as the would-be shaman sulked by himself at the edge of the circle. "I saw you wearing a piece of bone in your face earlier today. Is this the new fashion of your Spotted Ponies Clan?"

Several braves laughed. But the disgruntled Wolf Who Hunts Smiling was never one to admit defeat.

"You mock, fools! Were you present when this shaman set a star on fire and sent it across the heavens? Do you deny this?"

His words were greeted by silence. For they

contained a hard nugget of truth. Everyone had indeed seen this thing.

Once again Touch the Sky chafed. For he could not reveal the truth without placing Honey Eater in mortal danger.

"This thing today," Wolf Who Hunts Smiling continued. "You all say it was Woman Fa—Touch the Sky's big medicine that saved us. Only, think on this thing. Did he bless this mountain lion skin? Was his magic involved? No! This skin was given to him.

"And truly, how do you even know the mountain lion skin is blessed with strong medicine? Maiyun reveals himself in strange ways. It could well have been Medicine Flute's bone instrument that cast the magic aura about Touch the Sky. Stranger things have happened."

Most ignored him, returning to their dance. But later, as Touch the Sky turned his bay out to graze with the rest of the herd, Wolf Who Hunts Smiling caught him alone.

"Gloat, Woman Face. In the Panther Clan we have a saying. The worm turns slowly, indeed, but it always turns. Best have eyes in your back. I once walked between you and the fire. I have not taken back that promise to kill you."

Touch the Sky met his enemy's furtive, swift-as-minnow eyes.

"You are a murderer, Panther Clan. You have shed the blood of your own, and I no longer consider you a Cheyenne. I will not kill you in cold blood while you sleep, as you would kill me. But count upon it, I will kill you."

173

Wolf Who Hunts Smiling grinned, clearly enjoying this. "Then we understand each other?"

Touch the Sky nodded, his mouth a grim, determined slit. "We understand each other."

"I will enjoy killing you, shaman. You are a worthy enemy."

"Is it so? As for me, I will not enjoy killing you, for I consider you a pig's afterbirth, not a man."

The grin faded from Wolf Who Hunts Smiling's eyes, and rage twisted his face. Now it was Touch the Sky's turn to grin.

"Look. Even now the woman shows her feelings in her face," he said, borrowing one of Wolf Who Hunts Smiling's favorite taunts.

Still grinning, Touch the Sky walked away to join his fellow warriors in the victory dance.

CHEYENNE

JUDD COLE

Born Indian, raised white, Touch the Sky swears he'll die a free man. Don't miss one exciting adventure as the young brave searches for a world he can call his own.

#1: Arrow Keeper.
__3312-7 $3.50 US/$4.50 CAN

#2: Death Chant.
__3337-2 $3.50 US/$4.50 CAN

#3: Renegade Justice.
__3385-2 $3.50 US/$4.50 CAN

#4: Vision Quest.
__3411-5 $3.50 US/$4.50 CAN

Judd Cole
Follow the adventures of Touch the Sky as he searches for a world he can call his own!

#5: Blood on the Plains. When one of Touch the Sky's white friends suddenly appears, he brings with him a murderous enemy—the rivermen who employ him are really greedy land-grabbers out to steal the Indian's hunting grounds. If the young brave cannot convince his tribe that they are in danger, the swindlers will soak the ground with innocent blood.

_3441-7 $3.50 US/$4.50 CAN

#6: Comanche Raid. When a band of Comanche attack Touch the Sky's tribe, the silence of the prairie is shattered by the cries of the dead and dying. If Touch the Sky and the Cheyenne braves can't fend off the vicious war party, they will be slaughtered like the mighty beasts of the plains.

_3478-6 $3.50 US/$4.50 CAN

#7: Comancheros. When a notorious slave trader captures their women and children, Touch the Sky and his brother warriors race to save them so their glorious past won't fade into a bleak and hopeless future.

_3496-4 $3.50 US/$4.50 CAN